The Shack Out Back

By

John Hash and John C. McCurdy

TABLE OF CONTENTS

Our contributing authors:

Carter Taylor Seaton is the award-winning author of two novels, Father's Troubles, and amo, amas, amat...an unconventional love story, numerous magazine articles, and several essays, short stories, and the non-fiction, Hippie Homesteaders (WVU Press 2015.) Her biography of the late Congressman Ken Hechler, The Rebel in the Red Jeep, was released by West Virginia University Press in 2017. Her latest book, Me and MaryAnn is a compilation of stories of her mischievous childhood and youth. She is also a regular contributor to Huntington Quarterly Magazine.

William M. Ward is a "baby boomer" born in the 1950's in southern West Virginia to parents that lived all their lives at that point in the rural settings of Appalachia then migrated north to northern industrialized Ohio when he was 3 years old to pursue the jobs of the day.   Having spent 30 years in consumer electronics repair William is now retired and has relocated to Lewisburg, WV. He has been an avid book reader since learning to read and has always had hopes of writing and publishing some short stories or poems for the enjoyment of others. As is usually the case, hopes and dreams most times take a second seat to earning a living, so his writing has had to be delayed until he had the opportunity to spend the time required to produce the poems, short stories and articles. Now he has the opportunity to share his work with everyone.

John L. Hash is a writer and publisher from Huntington, West Virginia. His eight book Lero Series involves a secret agent working directly for the President. His other works include "Honey Branches: The Meade Estate," and "Starkeeper," a book of short stories about aviation. His Appalachian Anthology, "The Shack Out Back," co-authored by John C. McCurdy, is his latest.

John C. McCurdy is retired and lives in Alderson, West Virginia. His father was head of maintenance at Virginia Military Institute, which gave John his early interest in history, particularly military history. He was a career corrections officer at the Women's Federal Prison, near Alderson, and that provided him with many characters to study and write about. John has written numerous articles and short stories, most of which have been published in the Aldersonian, the newspaper for Alderson, West Virginia.

Cindy Black, a proud veteran of USANG, lives on a small farm in NE Kentucky. They raise Hereford x cattle, own Blacks Camper Lots, and Blacks Bookshop. The Bookshop Robbery was her first published short story. She is currently working on her first novel.

Michael Connick was born and raised in San Francisco, CA. During a career spanning much of the Cold War, he served as a consultant to various branches of the US intelligence community and the Department of Defense. His work took him all over the US, Europe, and the Middle East. He now resides in the little college town of Huntington, WV. For more information, please see his web site: http://michaelconnick.com

Copyright 2019 Wiltshire Books LLC

All rights reserved. Previously copyrighted material used herein with permission.

This is a work of fiction and any resemblance of any character to any person living or dead is unintended and purely coincidental.

The Shack Out Back

by William M. Ward

I don't remember the first time I saw the shack out back, but I remember the first time it saw me. Yes, I said that correctly, it saw me. I know, it sounds crazy and perhaps it is but crazy or not, it happened.

Now there is nothing unusual about this small building structure sitting in the back corner of the property that I own. It was apparently a storage shed at some time in the past. I never gave it a second glance when I acquired the property and I didn't bother to explore it till after I moved into the house.

I had only lived on the property for less than a month now and I was trying to adjust to a new place. You know how that is. Unpack this here, put this there. It was a tough job for a guy alone. I was also trying to adjust to being alone after ending a 24 year marriage to my high school sweetheart. Our union bore no fruit but we had been happy until Janine found herself. I guess that meditation instructor had something to do with that.....and he found her too. Several times from what I understand. So we got divorced and now here I am, Mark Weston, with my own place, alone again after 24 years.

The purchase of this property was done quickly with little thought to long term goals. I just needed to get away. So I got away, clear across the country from Northern California to Maryland. A radical change for sure but that is what I needed. With the sale of my property in California and some very lucky investments in some stocks I had enough money to last me at least five years even after buying the property if I didn't go nuts on the spending.

My job with a research and development firm had also gone very well in the past 15 years so I had some income from the products I helped develop for them. At 49 years old I am essentially retired with a comfortable living and time on my hands.

Time.....just what I need when I have to think about all the bitter moments of the last couple of years. The hurt is still there but hey, I am working on it. I have dated some but I just can't get into that scene yet. Too much, too soon.

So for now, I have a new place to work on, all this stuff to put away, some minor things to repair, some new neighbors to meet (my nearest neighbor is at least 3/4 mile away in one direction and 1 1/2 miles in the other). Then I got the shack. The shack. That damn shack that looks at me and sees me. I know it does! I feel it!

The shack itself looks to be about 20ft X 8ftX 8ft. It has a sharply slanted metal roof, some type of panels for walls and doors hanging open with a dark maul of an opening that you can't see into. There are briars and brambles and small trees, bushes and all manner of weeds and growths around it. It hasn't been used since who knows when but I know it is alive. The darkness in the doorway is impenetrable except when the light appears. It has a shimmering, wavering violet hued vortex with what appears to be eyes floating in it. It can see me when I get too near to it and I have seen it.

I know, you are thinking that I am crazy but I swear to you that I am not. I am going to go out there and try to figure out what this thing is and why it is watching me. I will go this afternoon.

Man! That was close! I thought for a second that it had me. I know....I need to settle down, catch my breath and tell you about it in a calm detailed manner but Holy Crap! Ok.....I'm ok. Here we go.

I had prepared (I thought) for my little foray out back by taking along a flashlight, a 25ft. length of rope and a tire iron. I am still not sure why I took the tire iron but it seemed like a good idea at the time. I don't know what I thought might come out of that shed that I would have to use it on but if something did, I wanted to be ready. I had approached the shed or shack or whatever you might call it with all due caution. If anyone had been watching me I know they would think I had lost my mind but at the moment I didn't give a damn. This was my life (did I really think in terms of my life) and I wasn't taking any chances. When I was within about 15 feet of the front side of the shack with the doorway blackness yawning I stopped, looked and listened. I couldn't see a damn thing inside even though the afternoon sun was shining brightly. The blackness seemed a solid mass and impenetrable. I steeled myself and stepped closer to maybe 7 to 8ft. from the doorway. There was still no details that I could make out inside so I thought I would be brave and I stepped right up to the doorway. OK...here I am now standing at the threshold of discovery, where is my reward? Still nothing.

I threw back my head and said "HAH!". Making fun of my fears could help me get over them I guess since nothing was happening. WRONG MOVE!! Suddenly a small violet hued spot appeared in the middle of the inky blackness and rapidly grew to about 10ft. in diameter. Swirls appeared in the circle making it look a lot like our pictorial representation of a swirling galaxy with its spiral arms. Located in the upper section about 3/4 of the way up there opened what appeared to be wispy eyes and they were looking AT ME! My breath caught in my throat. This had all happened in the span of maybe 3 seconds and I had not even time to move and when I tried I found that I was rooted to the spot. I took all this in in an instant noting that there were no other facial features other than those damn spooky eyes. I stood there staring into those eyes seeing the pain and misery that lurked there. The eyes were no particular color, they were like mere outlines within the swirls of the violet mist of the vortex but the suffering was there, very plain, very stark. Those eyes pleaded for help, pleaded for MY help. What could I do? How could I do anything with that misty substance, that viscous swirling substance of the cosmos?

I then remembered the rope and the tire iron. I thought that if there were someone trapped within that mist perhaps by throwing them a rope I could pull them out and that way end up a hero! So, being the brave stout fellow that I am I tied the rope around the tire iron and took the tire iron in hand, made sure my rope would feed properly and let it fly. The iron arced out gracefully through the air and when it reached the misty swirl the solid form of the metal of the iron took on a shimmery ghostlike appearance then entered the mist just below the eyes. BULLSEYE! (So to speak.) There was a coldness that shot up the rope and into my hands that was so unexpected I almost dropped the rope. The forward motion of the iron seemed to have stopped but I had not felt a thud of it landing or anything other than the intense coldness. I braced myself to give a big yank on the rope by wrapping the rope around my forearm several times. All of a sudden the rope pulled me nearly off my feet causing me to run across the lip of the shack door a couple of feet into the building then I caught my footing and planted them against the floor and pulled back for all I was worth. Just for a moment I was convinced that I was going tumble into that horrible coldness. I gained my footing back enough to get some slack and dropped the rope. I can tell you now that the tug of war going on in the shack was as close as I ever want to come to losing anything in my life. At that moment I glanced at those eyes and what I saw absolutely terrified me beyond all measure. They contained what I would call pure glee. I could not have been mistaken about this at all. I was certain that they had suckered me into this situation and I do not know why but the why really doesn't matter. I had only avoided becoming its next victim by the skin of my teeth. I finally found my feet and turned and ran like the seven Hells were pursuing me and perhaps they were.

I know that my ordeal in the shack is not over. I must do something about it or who knows what could happen? I don't want this responsibility but who else is there? Who else knows what I do? I just have to figure this out.

OK. I think I have a plan. I am not going to detail it here until I get back from the task of ridding the world? worlds? (what would be the right terminology I don't know) of this thing. Wish me luck.

Excerpt from Crofton-West County Gazette

Local- The Chief of Police announced today that they are in an ongoing investigation into the disappearance of county resident Mark Weston who had moved here a short time ago from California. The Chief says that Mr. Weston was reported missing after relatives from California failed to reach him by telephone and neighbors tried to raise him by knocking on his doors. Mr. Weston's home seems intact with nothing missing and it was as though he just walked out and vanished into thin air. Police conducted a thorough search of the property and surrounding area and found nothing. One Deputy did say that while searching the back part of the property near an old run down shack that he had thought he heard a faint call for help from inside the building. After he looked inside and found nothing he determined that he had probably not actually heard anything at all. There was an unusual ozone type smell from around the back area of the property but they could not link that up with any reason for the disappearance. The investigation is continuing.

Copyright 2014 William M. Ward

The Red Pickup

William M. Ward

Mary sat in the passenger seat of the pickup truck waiting for Tom to get back. He had told her to wait in the truck for him. They were parked in a dirty old junkyard that Tom had come to to look for a part for his new (well, new to him) 1962 Chevy pickup truck that he had bought just the week before. It was a beautiful cherry red and in pretty good condition even if it was 3 years old now. The interior was almost flawless and Tom had scrubbed and cleaned the vehicle so it would look its best for their date. Tom had left the keys in the ignition so Mary reached over and turned the key just enough to let the radio play. She scanned the dial looking for a good rock-n-roll station hoping to hear another great song by The Beatles. She loved their music, it was different than most music being done in the U.S. these days and she also liked the new look they brought with them from England.

After going thru the whole AM band she could hear nothing but static so she switched off the ignition and sat waiting, getting bored. Since they were supposedly on a date she thought they were going to the drive-in hamburger stand to get a burger and fries and then going to the movies afterward. Instead, Tom had driven directly here and here she sat starting to get irritated for being kept waiting.

While waiting Mary observed a young man, an employee of the junkyard no doubt, come along the row of junked vehicles apparently looking for a specific one. He found what he was looking for and proceeded to start removing engine parts that they could sell. She noticed that he turned his head and looked at this pristine red pickup sitting there with a curious look on his face. Shaking his head he turned back and resumed his task.

Mary looked down at her new dress she had bought earlier in the day and she smiled knowing that she cut quite a figure in that new dress. It was a dusty rose color and went well with the cherry red of the truck. She knew Tom liked it from the way jaw dropped when he had picked her up at her house. He had opened her door for her as a gentleman should and when she was stepping up into the truck he gave a low whistle of appreciation. This made her smile again as she sat there thinking about it.

Mary looked around to see if she could spot Tom anywhere so she could signal him to come on. She could not see him anywhere. If she had to get out of this truck and go find him he would have some tall making up to do when they did get this date going. Fuming, she reached for the door handle and pulled. Nothing happened, it would not open. She jerked up on it very hard not caring if she broke it or not but still....nothing. Scooting over to the driver's door she pulled up on the handle but the door remained shut. Now she was scared, not sure what to do.

As she sat there thinking about the situation there was a crackling sound from the dash. As she watched there appeared cracks in the dash like those that happen when the interior of the vehicle was exposed to direct sun for long periods. The cracks kept advancing and now cracks were spider-webbing through the glass of the windshield. The handles that she had so recently tried to use to open her doors faded into nothingness. The steering wheel also disappeared and now the glass on the

16

passenger side of the windshield fell away to expose a large hole in the glass. Mary was extremely frightened and did not understand what was happening. Looking down at her dress again she saw that the material of the dress was degrading before her eyes until it appeared to have been left in the open for many years. Looking out the also broken side window to the side view mirror and seeing her shocked face with her eyes growing wide with fright she saw that her face looked pale and drawn and was covered with blood...........

Joel finished removing the requested parts from this old Ford he had been dismantling. As he turned once more to look at the old rusted red Chevy pickup truck he could have sworn he saw a pale face staring back at him from inside the cab of the truck. He once more marveled at how the setting sun shining off the front window where a huge hole was how it looked like blood was splashed all over the glass and the hood of the truck. Just an optical illusion he knew but still.........

Mary watched with tears in her eyes as the junkyard and all the old junk cars around her faded from sight. She then remembered how her date night that had taken place 50 years ago had ended with a horrific crash as they were leaving the junkyard. They had not seen the Greyhound bus that was barreling down the street.

Mary longed to join her parents and other friends that had gone on to their afterlife but after all.......Tom had told her to stay in the truck.

Fog on the River New

Early every morning on the river New,

Fog hangs low over the water and the land,

Spreading forward and obscuring the view,

Of the New River and sights so grand.

Eons have passed since it began to flow,

Being one of the oldest in the world,

Just so we are privileged to know,

The sight of those waters that swirl.

Providing the people with all things they need,

Flowing through the mountains so majestic,

So development of man could proceed,

To build a life and home domestic.

Times have progressed to the present,

With life on the river going on,

Being along the shores and so content,

To see the fog at the crack of dawn.

Copyright 2016 William M. Ward

I've Got To Get Out of These Clothes Fast!

John Hash

2014

Things did not go anywhere near like I planned. Here I am stuck in my apartment, with blood spattered clothes, a bullet hole through the left sleeve, and surely some powder residue somewhere. Damn! I sure didn't think he would see me, but I guess with my loss of hearing, I was making more noise than I thought. Sure is funny how things turn out. I was ready to shoot him in cold blood, alright. What he did to those kids deprived him of any mercy. But it sure did not turn out the way I thought it would. I had not expected him to be armed, either. Now, I have blood spattered clothes, with powder burns and a bullet hole. The bullet passed through the inside of my left sleeve. A couple of inches east and I would be in serious trouble. Deep breaths. Calm down!

When he rose up and turned with that gun in his hand, there was only one thing to do. Sure was lucky that his shot missed, but it was close.

Now what to do? That time in the Military Police in the service needs to kick in.

First get the clothes off. Quickly, now, but deliberately and carefully. All of them, even underwear. Put on rubber gloves. Check shoe soles for blood spatter. If any, wash floor where I walked with strong salt water solution. Throw bucket of cold, salty water on sidewalk and hose off, too, after dark. Soak shoes in strong salt solution, then throw them away at first opportunity. Flush solution down toilet. Then put clothes onto a sheet of newspaper. Cut clothes into flushable pieces, even the belt. Flush handfuls at a time. Tear newspaper to shreds, then flush pieces. Then flush rubber gloves.

Take a long, hot, soapy shower, wash hands with kitchen abrasive cleanser first. Shampoo hair thoroughly. Powder residue might have accumulated there. Blow nose vigorously many times, too. Brush teeth after rinsing with mouth wash. Spit in commode. Rinse shower down with strong salt water solution after.

Good thing I kept that throw away revolver all these years. No one will ever miss it. Wipe it down with oily rag. Wrap in newspaper for later disposal.

Next thing is to discipline myself to remain calm. I know I will have to answer to the Lord for planning to shoot him like that, but since he was armed and shot first, maybe the Lord will shorten my time in hell.

At least he knew, in the briefest of intervals, why I was there and why he was going to get his. He won't be bothering any more kids where he is going.

If his body is found any time soon, they will know right away that the bullet in him is not from his revolver. But, on the other hand, I don't know if the bullet went clear through. Time was too short to check. If it went clear through, they may not find it. Finding his gun in his hand may divert them into a suicide theory. He surely had enough to be guilty about to take his own life.

If, on the other hand, the initial belief is homicide, the police will be pursuing everyone with motive. Funny how the initial impression about whether a death is a suicide takes on a life of its own and it is hard to change. Even though I was just a neighbor, I will probably be questioned. He lived in the next block, so it probably will be some time before they come to my place, if they do.

People are going to be surprised to find out that he was an unregistered sex offender.

The neighborhood's problem with him is over. Nothing can undo what he did, though. Now the problem is mine. Maybe it would help calm me down if I would fix a nice cup of coffee and work on Sunday's sermon.

The Book Store Robbery

By Cindy Black

The rain splattered against the window panes of my bookstore on a dreary November day. It was located in Ironton which is a sleepy little town in southern Ohio along the edge of the Ohio River that winds through the Appalachian foothills. It was a cold rain the kind that teased your mind with maybe or maybe not it might turn into snow. I wasn't sure about opening this morning. People generally don't get out and about in this kind of weather. My sales were low and opening wouldn't cost me anything since I was working. So I crawled out of my nice warm bed where I left my husband, Mark, who also serves as my foot warmer, and came in.

The drive takes me about 20 minutes. I try to tune into a local AM station to get the latest news from a talk show host, Tom Roten, the "Straight Shooter". He usually gets my adrenaline flowing on some topic of disgust. This morning it was about all the crime and why the criminals choose to wear hoodies all the time. Is it some kind of gang, or just individual thugs? Most of them wear their pants down to their knees too, exposing their dirty underwear. I mean, my goodness. Really?

By the time I opened the store, I was ready for something positive. After I tuned the radio to Walk-FM, my favorite Christian station, I poured a fresh pot of Old Village Roaster Columbian Supreme coffee in the coffee port for my customers as I hoped they might get bored at home and venture in to chat and buy a book. I knew most of my customers on a first name basis. Every now and then an out of town visitor would drop in.

They were usually staying in the one of the two new hotels that were recently built beside the state highway. They were the big spenders. But mostly my sales were from local people. I also had quite a few customers from across the river in Kentucky. After the big Amazon craze, bookstores have become scarce. So, I decided to take a leap of faith and open one up a couple of years ago. It has been a struggle. People do not understand the importance of shopping local to keep their community running. They cannot comprehend that sales tax is the revenue that pays the city workers, fire department, police, jail, garbage workers, and Mayor. It's hard to get people off their couch and come to the down town area. But a few local business people have gotten together to form an Ironton Business Community group to help revitalize the down town. Tonight they were having a meeting at the book store.

As I looked around the shop, I made a mental list of things I needed to get done this day. The new book order must be submitted to the book distributor today so the books would arrive before the weekend. I had some books from a new consignor I needed to clean, log into the database, then get on the shelves. Dixon, our tiger striped book store cat, needed his litter box cleaned, fresh water and food.

Dixon was a trial. One of the employees suggested getting a cat for the book store. "It's all the rage in Japan" she said. Without thinking, I agreed. We ended up with a cat with one leg in the grave, very thin, came with an abscessed tooth, and shed something horrible. So, we were stuck with him. I told her we should have looked at him before we agreed to take him. But he has such a sweet disposition, so we decided to love him anyway.

But right now I wanted to straighten up some huge art books on a bottom shelf near the back of the store. I had a customer the previous day with whom I had gone through them and we left it in a mess, so I wanted to get that job out of the way.

I walked back and knelt down so I could still see the entry way, a habit I unconsciously taught myself. I had not invested in a door buzzer at this point. The books were heavy, Picasso, Rembrandt, Monet, and others. I love these books. I could spend hours going over the beautiful art work hidden inside each one of them but I never have had the luxury of time to enjoy them.

As I was working, I began to hear squeaky steps from wet rubber soles on the black and white checkered tile floor. Dixon, who is somewhat of an alarm when anyone enters, whizzed by me. I stood up to see who it may be and let them know I was present. I saw a scrawny young man, about five feet four in a black hoodie, and a faded pair of blue jeans. Instantly, my mind flipped back to what the "Straight Shooter" was talking about the hoodie criminals on the radio before I arrived this morning. When he saw me, he put his shaky hand into his front pocket, pulled out a black snub-nose revolver and pointed it at me. This caught me totally off guard. Never would I have dreamed this would happen to me. I froze.

Then he said "Give me your money!" I could not help myself and burst out laughing, throwing my head back, and slapping my thigh as my eyes began to water from laughing so hard.

This caught the would-be robber totally off guard. He looked at me disbelieving and commanded again in a somewhat irritated and aggressive tone "I said, give me your money!"

Well, I just doubled over then I was laughing so hard.

His look of disbelief immediately turned to an impatient angry look. He said "What's so funny? Don't you know you're being robbed? I'll shoot you!"

After I got my breath and wiped the tears from my eyes I said "I'm sorry but number 1 your pocket you pulled that gun from is soaking wet and it's dripping water from the barrel. Number 2 you're on camera. Number 3, I don't have but 10 one dollar bills in the whole place."

I started to laugh again as I began to walk toward him.

"If you're looking for money, I'll look with you."

His angry face turned a deep red from embarrassment. He threw his plastic squirt gun so hard on the floor that it shattered into several pieces. He began to stomp out the door.

I said "Hey, hey, wait a minute. Why are you wanting to rob me?"

He hesitated before he opened the swinging glass door to exit.

I said "If you're hungry, I got some food in the back room."

He turned around with a stunned look on his face. He said "I haven't eaten in three days" solemnly as he looked down at his feet.

"I thought you looked a bit thin & shaky. I guess you've come to the right place. I'll get you some food and you have a seat."

He sat down and pulled the hoodie off his head as I went to fetch some food for him. I grabbed the bologna & cheese sandwich I had brought for my lunch, a banana, a thing of yogurt and put a cup of water in the microwave so I could make him a cup of hot chocolate. I got a fork and spoon as I walked back to the front of the store where he sat. I put the food in front of him and I could see he was just a kid. I told him "eat slowly so you don't get sick". Then I went back to fix his hot chocolate.

He had eaten the banana first and now he was smelling the sandwich. He could see the puzzled look on my face as I watched him. He said "After eating out of dumpsters so long, I've learned to smell food before I eat it. Now it's a habit".

I said "Oh, well that makes sense" as my heart felt a wave of sympathy and compassion for him."

"How old are you"?

"I'm 15.

"Where do you live?"

"I got a sleeping bag in my knap sack. I sleep wherever I can find a warm place out of the cold.

"Where are your folks?"

"I don't know. I left last summer. Got tired of all the crap. They thought more of their drugs than they did of me. Figure I'm better off without them."

"That's a big statement for a 15 year old. You know there's a shelter over on 5th & Park where you can sleep, right?"

"No. I didn't know. But if I go there, they will turn me in to the authorities. I don't want that. I can make it on my own."

"Oh. I see. Well, believe it or not, I understand. When I was your age, I felt the same way. My parents didn't do drugs, but alcohol. It makes people lose their sense of good judgement the Bible says!"

"The food is really good. I love hot chocolate. Can I take the yogurt with me?"

"You sure can. I tell you what, if you come by every evening, I'll have you something to eat" thinking to myself how I was going afford this.

"Really? That would be awesome" He said as I saw him smile for the first time.

"Well, we could do some trading. I need errands done occasionally like garbage taken out, windows washed, books mailed. So you could work for it so to say."

"Okay." He said. "What time do you close each day?"

"Usually seven PM depending on the weather".

"Well, I guess I'll see you tomorrow."

I reached under my shirt and pulled out a real snub-nosed 38 revolver as I watched his eyes grow big. "Next time, you better think twice before you try to rob someone. It's a wonder we're not scraping you up off the floor and putting you into a body bag." "You came real close to having a "Come to Jesus Meeting.'"

He turned and ran out the door. I wondered if I would see him again. Should I have said that? I wanted to get my message across to him. It was a bad choice on his part. But I didn't want to jeopardize the influence I might have. I guess tomorrow will be here soon enough to find out.

I called my husband and filled him in on what happened. "Are you okay?" he asked as I listened to the worry in his voice.

"Yeah but I wasn't expecting it".

"Well, you ought to come on home. Their saying a big snow is coming. 3-6 inches expected."

"You know it's a conspiracy with the grocery stores so people will do a "bread and milk run." Besides, I've got plenty to do here. I'll close up when I see the first snow flake."

"Okay. Love you" he said.

"Love you too" as I hung up the phone.

Then I began to pray. "Father, thank you that you took control of this situation and no one was hurt. I ask that you use me as you need to, to help that young man. Please keep him safe and warm and help his parents get their heads on straight. Restore that family and put your seal upon their hearts. In Jesus name I pray. Amen."

After all the excitement, I sat myself down to a cup of coffee. Memories of the morning's scare played havoc on my mind. "Lord, please speak your peace over me. Take away all the fear and confusion. You are Jehovah Shalom, the God of my peace. I love you Jesus."

I got up and went to the front where I had been and saw the first snow flake.

"I had better keep my word and close the shop up and head for home."

It snowed all evening and all night until we had 2" of snow by the time I woke up. The roads were clear by noon and off I went to Consigned Books. Downtown was buzzing as Thursday was court day. The court was held in the city building directly across the street from my bookstore.

I turn my open sign on and guess who came through the door? Yep, it was him. "Good afternoon" I said.

"Hi. Do you have something to eat? What do you need me to do?"

"First, I need you to tell me your name."

"Rocky" he said. "Rocky Meadows, and please don't laugh."

"Well, someone had a s0ense of humor" I chuckled. "I bet that's a hard name to live with."

"Yea. It gets old having people laugh every time I tell them my name. No one takes me serious after that."

"I can see why. There's some hot soup in the microwave. I didn't know if I scared you away or not."

Rocky went back and got it and he got the crackers too. I put coffee on, swept the floor, cleaned the glass door on the inside, and got a box of books to enter into the database. "Do you know how to use a laptop?" I asked.

"Yes, pretty good."

"What about excel? Can you use it?"

"No, but I can learn."

"Okay. That's all I need to hear." I let him eat and then began to teach him how to enter books into the database. This could be a blessing I thought. I sure needed the help. And I also discovered this young child needed a shower, desperately. How was I going achieve this great task?

Just then, my #1 customer, Paul Woods, came in for his daily cup of coffee. Paul was retired navy, a man I had grown to respect and love. He had become my advisor, my friend, and I considered him to be a legend. There were several legends in this little town that I had the privilege of becoming acquainted with. But Paul was the most consistent as far as showing his patronage support.

"Hey, Paul. Didn't think you would venture out today. Got someone here I want you to meet. This is Rocky Meadows" I said as he walked toward us.

"Hello. I think I've seen you around here. Have you found you some help Cindy?" He asked.

"I believe so. We're going trade labor for food."

"That'll work" Paul said.

Paul sat down at the table across from Rocky as I began to teach him how to enter each book into the excel spread sheet. It didn't take him any time to see how it was done. After entering several books with him, I let him go at it by himself.

"Hey Paul, let me get some advice on this window "I said as we walked outside. I told Paul how Rocky and I became acquainted. Then before he responded with anger, I asked him if he knew how we could get him a shower and clean clothes. "Paul's expression softened as he looked through the window at Rocky."

"Let me make some calls and get back at you. I'm glad you had your gun." Paul said looking at me over the rim of his glasses. "Never know when you might need it."

We walked back in and Paul left after he refilled his cup.

After Rocky entered all the books in the box, he asked if he could enter some more. This surprised me then I thought " eell he probably doesn't have anywhere else to go or nothing to do."

It was a lot warmer in here than on the street. So I let him get his quiver full with entering all he wanted to. He hung around all day and stayed busy as a couple of customers come thru. Right before I closed he got the bologna sandwich and headed out the door. "See you tomorrow" I said.

"Ok. Thank you" and away he went.

That night at home as I was telling my husband about Rocky, Paul called. "I know someone who can help with Rocky" he said. Then he began to fill me in on a place called "Nancy's Nook" in town that sells donated goods to fund their food pantry. So I called them. They agreed to come down the next day and get Rocky to go with them to get a shower and some clean clothes in exchange for a small donation. This sounded like the perfect plan until we could come up with a way to get him back in school.

I saw Nancy approach the door way and saw a surprised expression on her face as she stopped before coming in. I went outside and said "Nancy, what is it?"

"That's my grandson!" She said as big tears welled in her eyes.

"What! I exclaimed" You're kidding, right?"

"No. He's been missing for several months. No one knew what happened to him. My daughter and boyfriend are on drugs really bad. We don't have much communication with them. We could never seem to do anything with Rocky because she was afraid we would take him. I have been worried sick about him. I thought he joined the military or something. We've been praying so long."

"Oh my" I said. "What do you want me to do?" as we walked out of sight. "Would you want to take him home?"

"Oh yes! If he will go with me we would love to."

"I'll go ask him. You call your husband and make arrangements."

So I went back inside and sat down with Rocky. "I think we have a mutual friend, Rocky" I said nonchalantly.

"Oh, who is it?"

"Nancy Stumbo. Is that your grandmother?"

"Yes. But I don't think she likes me cause of all the drugs mom was doing. So I don't bother them."

"What if I told you they have been praying to find you? And they want to take you to their home?"

"Are you sure? They haven't seen me in quite a while. They don't know me very well."

Just then Nancy and her husband Mike walked in. Nancy came over to Rocky with tears in her eyes. "Rocky. Please come live with us. Cindy told us how you've been living. Honey, we've been so worried about you. Please, let us take care of you."

Rocky stood up as tears we're streaming down his face. "Grandma, are you sure?" Mike came over and hugged him.

"Yes, we're sure" Mike said.

I was beside myself. Thinking how I had prayed and ask the Lord to allow me to help Rocky. It all happened as if it was planned that way. I watched them walk out and Nancy turned and waved. I felt the Lord's peace fall on me and flood my soul with a joy unspeakable. Rocky stayed with Nancy and Mike, continued to work in my little bookstore after school, and went onto college. You never know what God will do if we just ask.

NO, NO, ANYTHING BUT THAT!

From <u>ProFUNdities</u>, by Phillip Clutts

Copyright 2011

(Be careful if you want to, but you're probably just wasting your time)

In one's efforts to undertake a task of some sort, advance recognition of the fact that one or more of the actions required to achieve the desired objective could - if improperly carried out - impact on the successful completion of the task in a very negative way, and of the fact that self-serving behavior on the part of inanimate objects in the proximate task area has an incredible potential to divert all of one's energies away from the task in order to deal with the hugely unpleasant consequences of said objects' contrariness, does not - in spite of all precautions - preclude the possibility that the outcome one wished to avoid at all costs will come to pass anyway, and may, in some perverse sort of way, increase the odds of an outcome that is totally unanticipated and even worse than the preconceived worst case scenario.

IDIOT'S DELIGHT

(Search me; I don't have a clue)

Phillip Clutts

From ProFUNdities, supra

2004

The joy and relief that one ordinarily experiences upon finally locating an item for which one has been searching in a state of considerable agitation over a considerable area for a considerable period of time is totally mitigated on those occasions when the item is discovered to have been in the physical possession of the searcher for the entire duration of the search or to have been precisely where it should have been all along.

On Cheat

John McCurdy

Copyright 2007

Some of my most loved memories are of camping with my sons and grandson on Cheat Mountain in Randolph County in West Virginia. On land belonging to the Moyer Lumber Company we'd spend ten days or so during the deer hunting season camped in this steep and rocky and almost primordial place.]

After the first year or so, we finally found the spot that for the next five or six years, we looked forward to visiting. With each years visits we became more and more familiar with the surrounding area. We camped in relative comfort, always in a camping trailer or a motor home with the conveniences of home we were accustomed to having in this spoiled life of ours. Nice hot meals, a warm and comfortable bed at night and even the niceties of electric lights to read or play penny-ante poker in the evenings.

With all this, when one stepped out at night and saw the sky without the lights from nearby cities obscuring the stars, when one felt the sharp, cold winds of October nights, and when, on rare occasions, off in the distance, one heard the scream of a bobcat or the dying cries of a creature destined to be the supper of a stronger predator, one could easily imagine being on the frontier in a time when life may have been simpler but was quite different in the intimacy with nature.

A hundred years ago the armies of the North and the South had minor skirmishes on the very ground we used, in fact, we were less than a quarter of a mile from the breastworks and trenches of the fortifications of Ft. Milroy, built to guard the road north toward

Huttonsville. The same distance in the other direction twelve or so Soldiers lay in graves nearly forgotten and barely visible in the underbrush!

Across the Frozen Lake

John Hash

2011

Unlatching the safety of an '03 Springfield rifle makes a distinctive sound, always has. Kind of like a "snick." I don't know what physical characteristic makes it distinctive, it just is.

The night is cold and clear. I am waiting behind an oak tree. In the distance a man is crossing the frozen lake on skis. In a few minutes he will be close enough. My instructions are that if he makes the wrong move at a particular time, I am to kill him. I don't know if I can do it.

The night is cold. And still. The birds have flown south. No wind blows. The old log hotel to my left is empty. Still he comes across the lake. My brother waits behind the next tree. This is his play. I am only a rifle here. He will talk to the man. If my brother raises his left arm, I am to shoot the other man. If my brother makes any other gesture, it means another thing. What am I to do? I have never shot a man before. But here we are, at a log hotel north of Morgantown, on the north shore of Cheat Lake, waiting for him to come. I don't know how I let my brother talk me into these crazy things. He said it is important. Life or death, he said. Something about a ransom. I am only to watch and do nothing unless he raises his left arm.

The moon shows on the snow, here by the oak tree and across the frozen lake. The Springfield nestles in my arm. It is hard against me. When I was younger, it didn't feel as hard. Maybe I was harder then. Still, he comes. My brother stirs and starts toward the man, keeping to the left, out of my line of sight. I guess where they will meet is two hundred yards from me. OK. No wind, easy shot. The man who is coming is only the messenger, I say to myself. He is only their minion. I won't shoot him unless he endangers my brother. If we can get some shred of information, maybe it will save Mr. Gallagher. We have to find him. His wife and family are frantic. How do I get involved in these things? He's only my brother's friend, I say to myself. Why do I have to shoot this man? Why can't my brother shoot him? He will be close. It would be easy. How do I let myself get into these things?

Aging Gently

John Hash

2011

I rattle and hack, cough and squeak

Snap, and groan and wheeze.

My back hurts, my feet hurt,

And I feel a twinge when I sneeze.

But, I love you.

It's late in the game, I can remember my name,

But some other things I forgot.

As foolish as it seems, I still have my dreams

And answer yes when you ask "You know what?"

But I love you.

No one can take from me the grip in my tummy

When you look at me just that way.

Though I'm getting spindly, I am still friendly

And I still respond when you say

I love you.

Is it time to put dreams away?

My last idea that failed

I'll be paying for it a while

I really thought it would sail

But I missed it by a mile.

Let's just put that dream away

Another may come to me yet

I'll trust in the Lord today

My path is His to direct.

What about that idea so good

Only yesterday, such promise and light

We could do it again, we could,

And that new idea seemed right.

So we'll sit on the porch and just rock

Grateful to be given this day

Without concern for the clock

Is it time to put dreams away?

Is it time to put dreams away?

Should we quit and just keep what we have?

Should we stop working each day

And give in to pain pills and salve?

So now we'll just dream and yawn

Tomorrow we'll talk of such things.

If we sleep on it, we'll see in the dawn

Our new idea sprout wings

Stay by my side and we'll abide.

I love you all there is.

Alderson Boys vs. Camp Greenbrier

(Or where the hell is the dock)?

John C. McCurdy   2005

A favorite leisure-time activity of the high-school age boys of Alderson was trying to find ways to make the lives of the young men at Camp Greenbrier for Boys as miserable as we could. The Camp Greenbrier guys were seen as upper-crust snobs from the tidewater section of Virginia, and many of them were just that. We viewed them as our rivals for the favors of the Alderson young women, and saw it as our duty to protect the ladies from the blandishments of the interloping rich boys from afar.

One Alderson boy, who lived just across the river from the Camp, would at odd intervals, row over during the campers lunch or supper hour, and steal everything that wasn't nailed down! Several other fellows who had strong throwing arms, delighted in standing outside the Camp fence and pelting the Camp area with rocks. Another bright young man found that, with his older brother's tennis racket, he could lob the hard pears from a tree on East Maple Avenue deep into the Campgrounds!

The owners of Camp Greenbrier weren't too cooperative in those years either, for example; they used the Greenbrier River for swimming and canoeing, but they did not, of course, have ownership of the River, however they acted as though they did, telling anyone who attempted to use the river near them to get out!

Bob Carter, Bunk Rowe, Bill Bryant and I decided that something needed to be done to make Camp Greenbrier know they were not the Kings of the River! We decided to cut free the large dock they placed each year, in the river to use as a swimming and diving and sunning spot! The dock, we imagined, would then float away causing confusion and consternation on the part of all Camp people, present and future, and enshrining us in the Alderson Hall of Fame as defenders of the community's honor!

We spent several days plotting and planning our operation. We were aware that the Dock was secured by cables running to large trees on the river bank, and that bolts and nuts were used to secure the cable to the dock, what we did not know was, whether or not the bolts and nuts were badly rusted. The Dock floated on a number of large metal oil barrels and had maybe two feet of space underneath. We could find concealment under the dock.

We knew that we must approach the dock from the water, we decided that the best way would be to enter the river above the Camp, near what was then known as the "Patton Swimming Hole", float through the rapids downstream and approach the Dock from the upstream side! One of us then would stay in the water almost at the bank and watch for any camp folks who might spread the alarm. The others would undo the nuts and bolts that secured the cables and free

the dock. We knew that the weight and size of the dock, (about 30 X 30 feet) , would prevent it from moving quickly and we would have plenty of time, after the Dock was freed, to then swim downstream to "Markley's Swimming Hole" now known as the "Alderson Mini-Park".

We needed transportation, we enlisted "Lib" Housby and took her into our confidence, and she agreed to help! A few nights later, in her Dad's Oldsmobile, she took us to "Patton's Swimming Hole", and dropped us off to begin our mission of reprisal!

It went like clockwork, down the rapids in the cool July water, floating, bumping along like four little innocent otters until we finally reached the head of the Camp Greenbrier pool and then very silently and vigilantly underneath the Dock. One of us had brought a wrench or pliers and the undoing of the first cable took only a few minutes. When it was released the Dock swung outward in the river and for a moment we thought the movement might cause problem or even an alarm from Camp. No problem. The last cable was loosened and we very quickly counted noses and ever so quietly began the long swim down to "Markley's".

Dear "Lib" was there to pick us up; behind the bushes along the riverbank, we changed into the dry clothing we had left in her automobile, then slowly, just as if she had been doing this sort of thing all her life, Lib drove us each home to the safety of our beds.

The next morning, of course, we couldn't wait to see what had happened to the Dock. It was wonderful; the bridge had many folks on it, looking down at one of the piers and wondering who or what had happened. A number of Camp Greenbrier Canoes were nearby, with the occupants scratching their heads . We were elated...

Bill Bryant slipped away from us, went up to Camp Greenbrier and got a job helping get the Dock back home, talk about making opportunities. He worked the rest of that summer. and several more at the Camp, a great example of opportunism at work.

Bob Craft

John McCurdy

Bob Craft and I go back a long way, in the 1950's Bob was at the Federal Prison Camp at Mill Point in Pocahontas County the temporary home of a pretty select group of Southern Moonshiners, Conscientious Objectors and other "good ole Boys". In case there may be a question, Bob was employed there! He got to go home at night!

The main work of the camp was harvesting the great mature hardwood of the National Forest in which they were located. There were no farm crops or gardens or livestock, just the Saw Mill and the woods crews.

As a result, for mutual benefit, Mill Point sent a busload of inmates to the Federal Reformatory for Women every day of the week, Monday through Friday in return for vegetables, fresh pork and beef and a lot of milk. You might think that their visits would pose some inter-relational problems and you would be correct. That would be subject for another discussion.

That's when I first met Bob Craft, the long, thin, son of a preacher, and who called Union his home. He was in charge of the inmates who came to Alderson to work. He would deliver the inmates to the various employees of the Reformatory who would actually supervise them during the day. Bob would then, for the remainder of the day, be the guardian of the Front Gate at Alderson. Since Mill Point was a man's institution not a lot of attention was paid to the fastidiousness of the officers, as long as they were clean and covered up it was OK, most men, you may know, think that is the way it should always be. But Alderson FRW was different and the Warden wanted her Male Officers to be sharply dressed with a capital "S"! Bob managed that quite well, he was really a fine looking first impression of the Institution even if he did not like it any more than any of the other fellows. That's when we became friends.

Later, after Mill Point closed, Bob was transferred to Alderson permanently. There were only nine Male Correctional Officers at the prison, and all of the jobs that were too distasteful for the female employees fell to which ever of those nine men was on duty. After responding to many, many calls to come stop fights or calm a group of inmates one became very trusting of ones fellows in crisis. A relationship not every man can enjoy among his fellows.

I could again relate the story of the building and the losing of a rowboat in the floodwaters of the Greenbrier, but that's been done. I might tell you of the very long winter when he and fellow employee Joe Henry Johnson expected to make their fortune by trapping the Beaver in the icy creeks of Kennison Mountain in Pocahontas County. How after enduring frost-bitten finger and near drowning's in those frigid waters, if they had only made a few more dollars they would have almost broke even!

I fished and I hunted with Bob Craft. We biked into the Cranberry wilderness and camped, we ate half raw bacon and burnt eggs, and once or so in our lives we shared the cup. I think we respected each other and enjoyed one another's company. We were young and we were going to live forever, it never seems to work that way and so once again I am saying goodbye to a friend.

I don't want to make Bob sound without fault, he sometimes had a head that was as hard as a rock, at times he could be a cantankerous cuss, as all of us men folk can, and as you ladies can attest. I call recall several time when our two hard heads clashed, but we fumed only a few hours and then we forgot it and went on.

Bob Craft was a decent, shy, humble man of wit and humor. He was a good and honorable man, a good husband and father, full of life and a lover of life. He was a lover of the outdoors, the smell of newly sawn wood and the burning leaves of autumn and of banjo music. A man's man, he was most of all a Gentleman and a Gentle Man. We should all do as well with our lives!

Boat-building on the Greenbrier

John McCurdy

2003

In the 60s' Bob and Charlotte Craft lived in what was called the Meadows House at the Federal Prison in Alderson. The house predated the Institution itself and was over in the hollow behind Cottages 2, 3 and 4; all now torn down to make way for a super-sized dormitory housing 500 inmates.

Let's just say the Meadows house was in the southeastern corner inside the eight foot tall fence that surrounded much of the institution grounds. Bob had been transferred to The Penitentiary in Atlanta when the Federal Prison Camp at Mill Point, West Virginia closed. He was from the Union area and wanted to get closer to home, he was transferred on the condition that he live on the institution grounds at the prison in Alderson.

Living in a Government house left Bob with a lot of idle time and we all know what the devil does with idle hands, do we not? Bob was used to the little creeks around Mill Point and Union and living near the Greenbrier was a real thrill for the lad! He decided to build a boat for the Greenbrier! He talked to anyone who would listen about the best kind of boat for fishing and all-around use and then he went to work on it.

He spent several months of his spare-time on the back porch of the Meadows House laying out and building a boat. A fine boat it was indeed, a flat bottomed John-boat that was about 14 feet long. He sanded and painted and drove everyone nearly crazy talking about that boat. At last it was complete, and he was ready to go see if his creation would actually float!

Bob, at the time, was the proud owner of an Oldsmobile 98 2-door sedan, it was a pretty thing and had a trunk big enough to ride a pony in, (and swing a lasso to boot)! Several days of hard rains and the Greenbrier was almost at flood-stage, since Bob wanted to tie his boat up behind the Institution Powerhouse, taking it there by water would be a lot easier than dragging it over the rail-road tracks and through the woods to the river. Bob loaded the boat into the cavernous trunk of the Oldsmobile and headed for the river.

Stopping at the Front-Gate to show off his handiwork, Bob said he was heading to put his boat in the river about where the Alderson Waste-water Treatment Plant is now located, and that he would accept help in doing so, if any would be offered. None was, but one of the smart-alecs, hanging around waiting for the quitting-time whistle, noticed that Bob had not as yet drilled the boat oars for the oarlocks and told Bob of the oversight.

Bob turned around and zipped back over to his house, in a few minutes, back out the gate he came, heading for the river.

In about an hour the Front Entrance Officer had a phone call from the Powerhouse Operating Engineer saying that Bob was there and asking if one of us would pick him up. When we saw Bob he was soaking wet and filthy dirty, scratches and cuts on his hands and face and all in all he was a pretty sorry, disreputable piece of humanity.

We were not about to let Bob get off without some explanation about what had happened. Seems he had put his oars into the boat, the boat into the water and then himself into the boat and then into the raging torrent of the Greenbrier in flood! Sitting down and putting the oars into position, he was dismayed to learn, that in his haste, he had drilled the oars and installed the oar-locks just exactly 90 degrees from where he should have. The oars sliced through the water quite nicely, just ineffectually! He tried to use an oar as a paddle but could do little to steer his boat in the fast-moving waters. He was finally able to get his craft into the trees behind the Powerhouse but was unable to stop! Reaching up and grabbing an overhead tree limb stopped the boat but that led to another problem, how to let go! Holding the boat against the current with his feet and legs was tiring, and suspending himself from a tree limb was fast becoming even more of a problem. To drop back into the boat would again leave him in the water without a paddle; to raise his feet would mean letting his prized boat go to where the flooding waters, and then how deep was the water he would drop into?

Finally at the end of his endurance he lifted his feet and sadly watched his boat float away, no chance of it snagging on a tree and stopping any way soon! At last, he dropped into the muddy water, which to his relief was only hip-deep, he struggled to the shore and to safety.

For a few days, the braver of us called him "Rowboat" instead of Robert, but since he was fast regaining his strength we quit flirting with disaster while we were ahead. The boat was never seen again as far as I know, and only now some 40 years later do I feel somewhat safe from Bob's wrath relating the story.

The Clock on the Mantle

John McCurdy 04

Our son Robert served on a Fast Frigate in the USN. That's not what this story is really about, just sort of incidentally.

One of out dearest friends was stationed at the Federal Reformatory for Women, here in Alderson, and we have remained close through the years since. We have shared each others joys and tragedies as friends do

Following his time here in the Public Health Service and a year in New Haven at Yale, Walt and his family settled into a practice at Narrows, Virginia. We were elated that they once again would be part of our life. My wife Pearl was pregnant and Walt agreed to be the deliveryman! Later he and his wife Barbara agreed to be our new sons God-parents! The next few years, were full of week-end visits to each others homes and the enjoyment of each others company. We were heart-broken when they told us they felt called to the Dominican Republic and the Peace Corp.

It was later after the death of his oldest son, the breakup of his and Barbara's marriage; his marriage to Sandi and moves to Santa Fe and The Puget Sound area, that Walt and Sandi returned to the East.

Walt's Mom and Dad, two delightful, retired school teachers from Queens in New York City, had decided to settle in south-eastern Virginia after they had been retired a few years. They bought a home in the New River Valley, at Pearisburg. They quickly became a part of the Presbyterian Church family and the rest of rural Virginia's good life. As happens they grew more and more infirm and it became apparent they would soon need Walt and Sandi!

It also was apparent that it would be much better if they were not uprooted.

So, Walt and Sandi moved to Virginia, Walt became part of the medical staff at VPI and Sandi began work on her MSW. The bought a house, and once again were Virginians! We were delighted; we visited back and forth every month or so, went to WVU-VPI ball-games and became once again acquainted with Helen and Walter, Walt's Mom and Dad. It is here the story really begins.

Walter Vom Lehn's father was a German immigrant who settled in Queens and became a successful homebuilder. When Walter finished High School at 18, he decided he didn't want to be a carpenter and he didn't want to go to college. He joined the Navy!

At the time of the completion of his boot camp training at Great Lakes, his group of trainees was asked if any of them would like to learn to dive. Walter raised his hand. In later years he told me he could do a fairly good jack-knife from a diving -board but he thought it would be nice to learn to do a half-gainer and a few of the more difficult dives of the spring-board!

In 1914-15, the navy did not have, as yet, any divers. Walter was in Class #1 of the USN school for Hard-Hat divers! He spent the rest of his enlistment cutting-up sunken Hazards-to-Navigation off the shores of the Outer Banks in North Carolina.

Returning to civilian life after WW 1, he went to Dartmouth College and on to become a teacher and administrator in the public schools of NYC.

When we met, we bonded, we were both Masons and we liked the same sorts of things. He told me of his childhood in NYC, and I told him about a farm-boys life in Virginia. I loaned him my books on Early American life written and illustrated so beautifully by Eric Sloan. He gave me an unused sharpening stone in a cast iron box that had been a gift to him when he was a Vocational Training Instructor. He asked me if I could make a sling like the one used by David to slay Goliath. I made him one from rawhide boot laces and the leather tongue of the same boot.

Helen died and his health grew worse, he came to live with Walt. When Walt and Sandi decided to move back to Friday Harbor in Puget Sound Walter came to live with us until his room and all its familiar furnishing could be moved to across the continent. When it was exactly as it had been on Virginia, my wife and I flew with him to his new home. He died peacefully in his sleep a year later. The sling was folded in his top dresser drawer!

The Seth Thomas clock on our mantle was a gift, from him, to a fellow sailor, our son Robert. It never seemed to us to chime correctly, and only after several years, did our son explain what the chimes really were.

It is a Sailor's Clock and it does not chime the hours, it chimes the "bells" of a sailor's duty on his "Watch". It tolls the 'bells' for seamen who in olden times could not afford a personal timepiece (i.e. a watch), they could thus determine if it were morning, noon, or night!

The end of a sailor's time on "Watch" was considered "8 bells", hence the saying, "Eight Bells and All Is Well"!

And so it is with Walter.

Communion

John McCurdy

2004

In one of my previous lives I was a Counselor in a Narcotic
Treatment Unit. One of the many supervisors of my training was
a psychologist who was much is demand in Human Relations and
other experiential counseling techniques. At his urging I became
a Trainer in Training with the Mid-Atlantic Training Committee, a
group based in Baltimore which provided help to organizations
and other groups who were in need of assistance.

We led a group consisting of Hollins College women, and other
persons from Roanoke who were in the helping professions,
over the Easter Holiday at the Episcopal Diocese Center in
Phoebe Needles, near Rocky Mount, Virginia. All of the
participants were   involved in the same organization in the
Roanoke area and that organization was experiencing some real
problems with staff and with communication among the staff
and volunteers. The sessions were from Thursday evening until
Sunday around mid-day.

We had divided the participants into two groups and I led one
group with a helper. The first night, Friday and most of Saturday
was disastrous, the group was unwilling to communicate on a
personal level and all of the trainers were at a loss. A
breakthrough occurred late Saturday evening and the

participants were so excited to finally be getting somewhere they decided they wanted to go all night if necessary. As often happens when people are sleepy and tired they let down the guards they have kept erected for years. Suddenly we had people talking about bad feeling they had held for years, imagined insults by others in the group that had never been addressed, let alone settled.

About 5:00 AM, we were finally over the crisis. One of the group suggested we go out side, we walked down and back the dark road, and somehow we ended at the long abandoned Chapel at Phoebe Needles.

As the sky began to lighten, one member of the group, a minister from Roanoke absent from his flock for this event said softly, "this is Easter Morning".

Things got very quiet, someone, almost under their breath began to say The Lord's Prayer. I think all may have joined in. One of the girls from Hollins got up and said, "I've got to go get something don't any of you dare leave". She ran down the road toward the center and in a few moment returned with three cold biscuits left from supper the night before and a bottle of cola she had discovered somewhere.

She announced, "I want to wash your feet and then I'm going to serve communion if I may".

And so as the sun rose on Easter Morning, we celebrated that holiest of days, The Resurrection of Christ.   We also celebrated the rebirth of a struggling organization.

"Ek " Carter

John McCurdy 04

Ek Carter was a drunk and a wife-beater! I was ten years old and I was absolutely fascinated by the man. He was short and ugly and unkempt and he threatened to cut off my ears with the large knife he carried and would pull from his pocket at almost any time. He terrified me, and yet at every opportunity I would slip away from home and go up along Kerr's Creek past the Carl Sensabaugh house and I'd visit EK.

Every other word he uttered was an oath and he was virtually an outcast among the staunch Baptist and Presbyterians in the rural community of Kerr's Creek, Virginia in the years of 1942-43. Ek's wife was a beaten-down, overworked woman, old before her time, who tried her best to keep the kids and home is some semblance of order with no help and much hindrance from Ek.

They lived in a ram-shackle house across from Jim Laird, (I think the Lairds looked upon them as their personal cross to bear). A falling down barn of sorts and several other rickety outbuildings graced the creek bank and backyard of the Carter home. A spare-ribbed milk cow, a few chickens that lived on their imagination and what the cow left behind, and a mean-tempered billy-goat were the other residents of the place.

On one of my furtive excursions to visit Ek I found him getting ready to milk. The cow was in the stall and Ek had finally found the milking stool he had thrown out in a fit of rage the day before. It was a one-legged stool and as Ek rocked his considerable bulk around getting in to the milking chore the one leg of the stool sank further and further into the built-up manure that made up the floor of the poor-excuse of a barn. Ek was finally sitting almost on the ground!

It was at this time that the Billy-goat decided to mess with Ek. Ek didn't take much messing with and he hit the goat with the handle of a nearby pitch-fork. The old billy-goat didn't take much messing with either and proceeded to get a running start and butt Ek in the back. The milk spilled, Ek sat down in the manure and the billy figuring he'd won, walked off.

He shouldn't have turned his back on Ek, exploding with curses; Ek grabbed the pitchfork and ran the tines through the goat's abdomen and chest. Leaving the pitchfork still sticking in the goat, Ek marched into the house cursing, probably to kick a few kids and slap his wife!

The next day curiosity took me back to the Carter house, no goat! The now affable Ek was in the back yard. "Boy, did you ever eat any goat meat"? He insisted I stay and eat with them. I didn't like the odor and I liked the taste of Old Billy even less. The Carter Family ate with gusto! I went home!

Dairy, Farm and Cannery

FRW Memories

John McCurdy 04

When the FRW first was envisioned, it was believed that healthy, hard, outdoor work was a good thing. Many, probably most, of the inmates sent to Alderson were obviously from rural areas since most of this country in the 20s and 30s was still an agrarian landscape.

The institution Farm was a vital part of the overall plan of the institution. To put women in a healthy environment with adequate health care, diets, and instill in them good work and personal habits and teach them modern, more productive ways of doing things was a goal. and they and their efforts would also be of great monetary value to the prison operation.

A dairy and vegetable truck gardens, and a Cannery to prepare and preserve the produce grown was part of that plan from the first days of the institution.

The dairy operation was as modern as could be seen, white-uniformed workers, immaculate surrounding and machinery to milk, chill, pasteurize and then bottle and deliver the milk to the kitchens of the prisons.

The Maples Cottage was a Federal Style two story building that housed the majority of the permanent inmate staff that was assigned to the dairy and the other farm operations. A clean, dry, well-lit basement contained the heating plant for the building and the facilities for the women to change from their work-cloths into clean garments. Upstairs on the first floor was a large kitchen and dining room, several offices, the officers' quarters and bath and a large Living Room with a piano and a radio, (remember this was before TV had reared its ugly head). The upper floor contained the inmate's rooms, most single occupancy but also several dormitories that four inmates could share. The toilet and bathing facilities were on that same floor. The attic of the building was a large, well-lit and high-ceilinged room that could have been converted into bedrooms if it were ever needed.

There was a tunnel under the main tracks of the Railroad to allow the cattle to move to and from the pasture land on the prison property between the river and the railroad. The majority of the institution gardening was also done in that area. During harvest additional inmates would be brought from the main institution to assist in gathering the crops.

When the vegetables had been gathered, truckloads would be delivered to the institution cannery behind the store house. My aunt, Mildred Fitzgerald Cumby, was often assigned there, with "her" inmates; they would wash, and prepare for the huge steam retorts and cookers the plethora of foodstuffs that were left at their door. Miserably hot, hard and somewhat dangerous work, but immensely gratifying. Somehow the majority of the women seemed to enjoy it, possibly because it was so much like what they did at when they were at their homes! I can recall my aunt always seemed happy when it was canning season. Tired and grumpy, but happy!

The women who lived at the Maples farm cottage attended all functions of life on the main campus such as school, religious services and the infrequent social activities. For the Friday night movies, the Male Correctional Officer on the evening shift would get the Storehouse delivery van, put several wooden benches in the back, always being certain that the benches were covered with Kraft wrapping paper from the storehouse to protect the Dairy Girls white uniforms from being soiled by the benches. (More about "the girls" term later!

We would bring the women in to the main grounds and later, of course, take them back out to their quarters. Getting them rounded up when time to go could often be a slow process, they may not have seen some friend for weeks and were reluctant to leave their company. The majority of the women who lived at the Maples always seemed to be of Spanish descent. Whether they were assigned there for a particular reason or whether they had expressed a desire to live and work there is unknown. My guess would be that it was a habit of the institution to assign Spanish women there because of their good work habits.

When the inmate population became more and more from the urban population centers and less and less from rural America: the average inmate was poorly educated as always, from the inner city and predominately black, the farm and dairy became less and less useful as a work skill for inmates and it was gradually phased out when the population of the institution dropped during the 1960s.

The farm was sold in the 60's and has been sold and resold several times since them, camping trailers now line the river bank. A turkey plant, a USDA Research Facility and small homes now occupy the acreage.

FRW Memories 2

(The Joy of Cooking)

John C. McCurdy   2005

The Federal Reformatory for Women in the 30's, 40's and even the 50's stressed the notion of a normal family life in their life skills training. The definition of "normal" was, of course that of the definer, and may have borne little resemblance to the actual life needs of the inmate   especially when one considers the upper middle class background of the Executive Staff.

In any event, "Home-Making Skills" were deemed to be need in the treatment program of many inmates, and a family atmosphere was a vital part of the early institution life.

Each group of two or three Cottages had one cottage with a Kitchen and a Dining Room to serve the others. Meals were eaten at tables for four persons, proper table manner and decorum were required of the diners, and even cloth napkins were used! Food was prepared on a large coal-burning stove that had to be lit each morning using kindling wood and paper to ignite the coal!

The Officer in the Cottage was required to rise at 5:30 AM, (they had spent the night in the cottage, in the room and bath provided for them), and start the fire in the cook stove, put on a pot of coffee and awaken her kitchen workers. They would then prepare breakfast for the rest of the women residing in the cottages.

Since the officers assigned to the kitchen cottages were not required to be good cooks and because many of the inmate were little better, an indispensable item in all of the Kitchens was a well-used, much food-stained copy of Rombauer and Beckers, "The Joy of Cooking"!

In the late 50's or early 60's a central kitchen and dining facility was built and the days of the Kitchen Cottage were over! With the large steam cauldrons and ovens now being used, there was little need for a two-quart sauce pan in the modern era of correctional food service. Old faithful pots, pans, skillets, ladles and serving dishes were stored in the Old Chicken House at the Farm, (with other no longer needed reminders of the past, they there, like "Little Boy Blue", waited!)

Cletis Shawver and I liberated most of the tattered copies of the "Joy of Cooking"

and made gifts of them to the officers who had spent much time in those kitchen cottages. My wife Pearl, although she was never in Food Service, has a copy, tattered and torn, a poor excuse for a book. For Christmas in 1973, I bought her a copy of the new addition, but her old copy has the place of honor among the several feet of cookbooks on her kitchen shelf!

Several years later, the surplus kitchen items stored on the farm were finally offered

for sale as junk. I bought all the smaller kitchen and serving pieces as a lot from the Junk Dealer, Surplus Navy silver -plate, au-gratin dishes, bowls, sugar bowls and creamers, tea pot and cocoa pots galore for $5.00! I enjoyed giving the pieces to those who knew what they were. I remember I gave "Sis" Simmons a large covered cream pitcher; she kept it on her coffee table.

FRW Memories 3

John McCurdy   04

In the spring of 1954, I began my career in the Prison Service. After 4 years at Radford Arsenal in Virginia. I had gotten the call that I thought might lead back to Alderson.

I had just recently been promoted to Shift Chemist and Supervisor at the Arsenal, shortly afterward, (and I can assure you I did not do it), the company lost several contracts because of the trouble they were having with the "Honest John", "Nike" and "Jato" motors they were producing for the U. S. Government. I had the feeling that since I was one of the few salaried persons in the Technical Department without a Degree, and since I only had seniority from the time I had been promoted, I guessed that I would be one of the first employees to be gone when the lay-offs began. Turned out I was wrong, the problems were solved, the contracts renewed and new employees hired!

I had previously taken the Civil Service test for Correctional Officer, and I had received a very high grade, in the year just past I had been called to several institutions and had refused appointment. The newly arrived letter offering me a Probationary Appointment at Ashland came at, what I thought was a good time! I immediately accepted and said I could report at the date they required.

I went to Ashland, Jimmy Johnson from Fort Spring, and I drove down and together and began our adventure in the Bureau of Prisons. It would be correct to say that when we drove onto the grounds of the prison and then into the Great Steel Doors of the Administration Building we were very apprehensive. In the next few days and months of Classroom training and on the job instruction with veteran officers my fears began to abate.

My first assignment, working alone, was in the 12-8 AM shift in a Dormitory. Being locked in with 100 or more snoring, dreaming, farting and who knows what else convicts, made me a little homesick for my previous job of making nitroglycerine and gunpowder. When The Yard-patrolman locked the door behind me and he left, I recall thinking, "what the devil have I gotten myself into and what am I here for?" Then I remembered what the OJT instructor had done and I began the very soon to be, boring task of walking, checking and counting! At 3:00 AM the Yard Patrolman came back and after going to the door and assuring him I was all right and not a hostage, he unlocked the door and let me out. Together we crossed over

to the next dorm and he let me in to cover the Count for that officer. I stood and watched while he counted to make certain that no inmate left his bed after being counted and slipped into an empty bed to be counted again to cover for an escapes inmate. After the Count was called in and it was okayed, we went to my dormitory and this time I counted. At times, as a learning experience, we were told that Count was wrong and to re-count! This was the Supervisors way of seeing if we were certain that our Count was correct. Every now and then an officer would adjust his Count to what he "thought" the Count was supposed to be. There would be some problems when that happened, the least being that the officer's Count would henceforth be a suspect! There was no room for guessing when it came to Counts in prison!

When the Count was over and we were again locked in, "Lord Above, we still had 4 hours to go until 8:00 AM! In those days we read all inmate mail, both incoming and out-going, it was opened and inspected for contraband such as drugs, razor blades, and stamps which could be used in an attempt to smuggle mail out of the Institution. Inmates in prison were notorious for playing on women's sympathy and telling each that they were the only girl the inmate would ever love, and attempt to get money sent in to their inmate account: sorry scoundrels that we were, we delighted in "accidentally" getting one ladies mail into another's envelope. Snickering as we imagined the trouble we were causing for the inmate!

The next three months I was assigned to Tower duty, if there is any more miserable job I don't know it. I worked something like two midnights, two evening and Saturday Day-shift. I remember coming to work one Sunday with the world's worst headache and upset stomach. (Much like a hang-over)! I vowed that if I could only live until quitting time I would never do that again. The entire inmate population could have climbed over the fence below my Tower and I would not have seen them, (and if I did see them there was no way I would have discharged that dirty old noisy gun in my condition!

Life got better, I left the downtown apartment I shared with three other rookies and moved to the Bachelor Officers Quarters at the Institution. Cheap rent, safe parking for my car, an inmate orderly to make my bed and tidy up after me, I ate my meals in the Officers Mess, good food for 25 cents a meal. I was going to Ashland College (was Instructor in the General Chemistry Laboratory for my tuition and other charges), played on the Institution softball team, went to the Pistol Range and shot as often as possible and all in all, was reasonable happy; except it was not home, Alderson where my wife and son were, and where I wanted to be was home.

I was the proud owner of a new Ford 2 door sedan; each week when my days-off arrived I could not wait to get on the road to Greenbrier County. Each week when I had to come back, I hated it more. But things were happening at the FRW in Alderson that would have profound effect on my future!

FRW Memories 4

John McCurdy 2004

When the transfer of Hurst and Harris became known in the Town of Alderson, an attempt was made to stop the transfers. A petition was drawn-up suggesting that the Town could ill-afford to lose such long-time residents. That didn't have a chance, the Warden of the FRW, Miss Kinsella's answer to the criticism was that those veteran officers were needed more at other institutions, and besides, two young men who were from the area were being transferred in to take their place! Jim White and I were those men!

I had gone to Ashland with the idea that in a few years I might be able to transfer to Alderson, and I applied for a transfer almost on the day I got there. I was very pleasantly nonplused when, while I was on my days off and in Alderson, Several people asked me how I thought I would like working at the FRW. My answer to each was, I'd like it a lot, but I'm afraid it will be a while. I finally made some calls and decided there might just be a chance the rumor was true. Another phone call to the Personnel Office at Ashland and I learned that the FRW had asked for my transfer to be effective on the following Monday! My family and I were elated, after nearly five years of working away, I was, at last coming home to earn a living.

I had lots to do in Ashland, I had to tell Ashland College of my transfer, gather up dry-cleaning and laundry and since it was already Thursday, do in one day what had to be done. I almost immediately drove back to Ashland. The next day was a whirlwind of paperwork, goodbyes and running here and there. The folks at Ashland were not awfully happy about the way things had happened. I found out later, that they had gotten a call from the Bureau Office in D. C. on Wednesday saying I was to report to Alderson the following Monday. Ashland's protests were of no avail.

I reported to work on Monday, I recall that Miss. Kinsella, when I we introduced to her said, "You're awfully young", and shook her head. I wondered if that was a very auspicious start. I recall that the supervisor in charge of the male Correctional Officers, Charles Keatley turned me over to the man I would learn to love, even while watching for his tricks and ruses! Joe Henry Johnson had transferred from Mill Point the previous year; he also was the man responsible for ordering uniforms for the men of the correctional force. The dark gray, double-breasted uniforms were made to order by the inmates in the Penitentiary at Leavenworth, Kansas: Rumor had it that they also provided the same clothing to the Veteran's Administration for the Burial of Indigent Veterans. Ashland did not order new employees uniforms until they were through the year's probation. Until then, we got the hand-me-downs of veteran officers. One of my coats had a repair in the back that had been the result of an inmates stabbing of the previous owner. Not exactly the sort of thing one liked to dwell on too much!

Joe Henry had the responsibility for much of my training the next few months. At that time the Male Correctional Officers worked a shift that changed every week, from days, to evenings, to the midnight watch. I was Johnson's shadow. I recall he took me to the institution greenhouse, which was filled with flowers and newly propagated shrubs, he told me before entering that Katherine Kelly and her mother, Ora Shannon worked there, and that Katherine was the wife of the notorious: Machine-Gun Kelly, who was serving life in either Leavenworth or Alcatraz. He cautioned me that Katherine was a manipulator and to be careful around her and her mother. They both were very engaging and answered every question very knowledgeably. Katherine insisted that I must see some of the Dolls she had made, when I said they were very nice, she insisted that I must take one for my wife. I just as insistently refused to do so. She feigned that she was deeply hurt!

At the Institution Hospital, which at that time was staffed by two Public Health Service Physicians and about 6 or 7 Registered Nurses, a PHS Dentist and a registered Pharmacist! Inmates received all their medical care, (including child-birth), at the institution. Iva d'Aquina, better known as 'Tokyo Rose" was assigned to the hospital; she was a very gracious individual, well liked by everyone. A few years afterward I was one of the people on duty when she was released. I was beginning the 12-8 shift and when I came to work was surprised to find a memorandum at the Front Entrance listing the names of all the well-known Media people who were there for her release the next morning. They began coming to the locked gate about 4:00AM that morning. Around 6 o'clock, additional staff began arriving including several of my fellow MCO's! Her brothers arrived to pick Iva up and they were allowed to drive, to the Administration Building with an escort, for her release. She made a statement to the press when they arrived back at the Front Entrance but she did not get out of the car. I went to her window and wished her good-luck and she in turn said simply, "goodbye, Mr. McCurdy, God Bless You", rolled up the window and left.

There was a tremendous difference in Iva D'Aquina, and others such as Katherine Kelly and "Axis Sally" or Mildred Gillars, who was a whiny, demanding sociopath who inmates and staff alike despised.

I worked my first 12-8 shift with Joe Johnson. After all the evening shift employees had left the Gate, we went to the Control Room, located in the Administration Building, chatted with the Control Room Officer and did a security and safety check of the building, with special interest paid to the refrigerators in the Staff Kitchen, which was then in the Ad. Building. Hopefully finding something good to eat!

We would then make the first of our walking inspections of the cottages on the Upper and the Lower Campus, we would, with our 5-cell flashlights inspect the screens of the rooms to make certain none were missing, torn or cut. Johnson once found an sheet hanging from an Upstairs window at "the Maples " farm cottage and phoned in that someone out there wanted to make "Peace", when was asked why, he replied, " because they are flying a white flag from the Second story window!" Few of the Higher-ups were amused!

The MCO would assist the Woman Officer assigned to Davis Hall (the building housing the inmates who were considered likely to "act out' or 'up'. Mrs. Vera Freeman was on the 12-8 shift in Davis Hall. She, also for some reason, had a room and bath there that she rented! When she did not wish to drive to White Sulphur Springs, she would remain at the institution and have a place to stay!

When we went to Davis Hall, Mrs. Freeman would always have a pot of coffee or tea and have cookies or other refreshment for us. We would drink and eat and chat and then help her make her count. That was done by the MCO unlocking the door and opening it, ready for whatever might happen. The Woman Officer would then enter the room if necessary in order for her to "see skin".

We would pick up a woman officer who had the job of Patrolling and go to the "Maples' cottage, which   was about a mile on the farm road from the Main Institution. While the woman officer checked and counted the inmates assigned to that cottage , we would check the Rear Gate, the Piggery and make sure the baby pigs weren't being suffocated by the brood sows laying on them, although what we were supposed to do if that happened I never knew! We would then return and park at the Maples and check the Dairy Barn and office and milk-room. The evening's milk was stored in large refrigerated, stainless steel vats awaiting separation and pasteurization by the Day Crew. The cold milk in the vat would have several inches of cream on it and we always got a paper cup and dipped about a quart of the Cream off to drink during the night! We picked up the woman officer and returned to the Institution proper. I remember that when we got to the locked Powerhouse Gate, the man would get out and unlock and open the gate and the Woman would slide into the driver's seat and drive the truck through.

We would check all the dark and silent building and about 4 a.m., go to the Main Dining Room and Kitchen and turn on the Ovens for the Food Service people who would soon be arriving to prepare the days meals.

The tall institution flag-pole was on the crest of the hill on the Upper Campus, as dawn broke we would get the Flag which was always properly folded and place on the radiator inside the end door of Willibrant Hall. The Flag was always raised briskly to the top of the flag pole as was proper! On the Night Shift the sound of the halyard clinking against the steel of the flag pole was reassuring for some reason. When the flag was lowered in the evening, it was folded as prescribed and reverently stored until the morning. There were no flag-burners working at Alderson!

For the rest of our shift we were letting staff in to work at various times until about 6:45, when we generally went to the gate to remain. Unless, of course, some inmate had gotten up on the wrong side of the bed and decided to create a disturbance.

Guarding Joe Valachi

FRW Memories 5

John McCurdy

In 1962 or 1963 I was called to the Wardens Office at The
Federal Reformatory for Women and asked if I would be
interested in volunteering for a special assignment for a two
weeks period. When I said I probably would the Warden
explained that the Bureau of Prisons had a special Inmate and
that officers were going to be assigned for two week periods to
the Federal Correctional Center on West Street in New York City!
The officers selected for thduty would be carried on a Special
Duty Roster at their home institution. They also were not to tell
anyone where or what they were doing. They would be on Per
Diem and also have other incentives for the two week period
they were on the assignment.

I said I was interested and would, indeed like the experience,
figuring it would be a good career move. About a month later I
was told that in two weeks I would be assigned to that duty!

When the time arrived, I drove to the Bureau Offices in
Washington, D.C., where myself and seven Officers from other
institutions were briefed on what we were getting into.

A member of the Mafia, was being held in the Metropolitan Correctional Center in NYC, and was going to testify for the Justice Department about his knowledge of that group. Because of the danger to that individual, he was going to be under the watch and care of a special group of officers.

Actually, they were afraid that the staff members of the MCC might be contacted and come under the influence of the Mafia, and that, in some way, either by threats or pay-offs the individual be unable to testify!

The witness was of course Joe Valachi, who had been an enforcer for the Genovese Crime Family for years. There was a price on Valachi and the persons who took his life before he could testify would be handsomely rewarded. In truth, that person's life would likely not be worth much as that individual could possibly tie the murder to someone!

We, all the special group, were driven from DC to the NYMCC in a regular Prison bus and entered the Center after dark and after most of the activity had ceased, we were taken up to the 9th or 10th floor by a special private elevator and shown to our rooms, (which were converted Offices).

Two officers were assigned to each room, and we became acquainted with the Facilities and that floors amenities. An attempt had obviously been made to keep us comfortable and happy. A day -room with a refrigerator and snacks, TV and a promise that if we needed anything we only had to ask. The shifts we would work were explained and we found that at midnight that Saturday two of us would be going on duty! We would not work Days except on the weekends. Valachi would be picked up each morning at 7:00 by Special Agents of the FBI, (who we found out later, were picked just as we were, for two weeks duty at a time)! Apparently the FBI in NYC wasn't trusted all that much either!

We would wake Valachi at 5:30, feed and shower him and get him dressed free-world (civilian) clothing, suit, white shirt, ties and all. After the FBI Agents took custody they were supposed to search and do it all over again before putting on leg-irons and handcuffs. They did so occasionally. At around 5:30 pm, they would return and after we had assumed custody, he would be taken into an examining room, stripped and his hair and body searched and a MTA, (now called a Physicians Assistant), would do a Body Orifice Examination, which always got a wise-crack from the generally cooperative and good-natured Valachi. He would be given clean under garments and coveralls and returned to his cell. The two officers assigned to the shift would generally be an attentive audience as he recounted the day's event, from his view point. Valachi was a natural wit, uneducated beyond the fifth grade he said, but with a great deal of street smarts. He delighted in telling us of his exploits, and never missed telling of all the mistakes he had made. He always made himself a victim of his own, as he called it, dumb wop ignorance. He was far from ignorant.

Although we received Per Diem for NYC which was even then about $100.00 per day our Quarters were furnished as were our meals. I did not go out while there. Two weeks later we were returned to DC for Debriefing and after retrieving my car from behind the Bureau Media Center and came home to Alderson.

Hunting Camp

John McCurdy 2003

The hunting camp was located on Douthat's Creek in Pocahontas County at the head of Three Mile Run and Devils Hollow. The poker playing and the late hours of the previous night had taken their toll on Jim Rowe, the intoxicant that the others had forced him to drink the night before had also had some effect upon his head and his stomach!

His head was big and it throbbed and his stomach felt even worse. 5 a.m. was way too early and the sound of the others belching and farting and eating food was enough to make a well man ill. The sound of the door slamming as the others went to the outhouse and behind the bushes near the cabins sounded like the start of WW 3, his head from where Grayson Housby had stepped on it sometime in the night as he got down from his upper bunk, was as sore on the outside as it was on the inside.

Jim announced to his fellows that he was going to stay in camp and clean up the filthy place and put on a pot of brown beans for supper, he might even make slaw and have cornbread to go with the beans.

Nature called sometime later and after a set-to in the frigid privy and exposure to the more or less fresh air therein, he decided to put some clothes on over his long johns, but the exertion made his head throb and he was forced to lay his tired body down.

After a short 3 hour nap he awoke with a start and realized he'd told his buddies he'd cook.

The water buckets were, of course, empty, someone, probably that damn sissy Shawver, he thought, had actually washed that morning! The spring was about two hundred yards up Devil's Hollow and there wasn't a darn thing to do but go get a bucket of two.

Putting on his old Ritchie Coat, he decided he might as well take his Browning 16, for a man in good health it was an easy walk to the spring, but to Jim the walk just made his head start throbbing again. At the spring, he brushed the leaves from the surface of the dark water and dipped in the buckets. His head hurt so badly and the water was so cool and inviting he lay down in the snow and buried his head in it, it felt so good.

He finally had to breath, raised his head and "God almighty "coming down the hill just in front of him was a flock of about 25 turkeys just a hustling. He pulled his Browning ever so slowly up beside him, and took dead aim on a big Gobbler with about a 12-15 inch beard.

Shawver and I topped the hill in pursuit of the turkeys just in time to see them spot Jim and fly crashing through the trees. Rushing down to the spring, Shawver demanded of Jim, " Dammit Rowe, why in the hell didn't you shoot and break them up, they would have flown right back toward us"?

Jim, in a defiant, yet chagrined and quiet voice said, "I had a bead on him and then I thought of the kick and the noise of that shotgun and I just decided to put my head back in the water"!

Dear Folks out on Kerr's Creek:

John McCurdy 05

Now that Martha is no longer a part of our little town, I guess we'll have to go back to hunting ginseng and trapping for excitement in our lives. I don't hear the words "Alderson" very often on the television set lately!

The "big city" TV crews and satellite trucks are a thing of the past, as is the sometimes 5 or 6 car back-ups at the ATM machine at the local City National Bank. One can again go in the local stores without being asked if we would like to be interviewed by the TV gang from Big Jaw, New Jersey.

The bottom line, after we get all the mileage we can out of the event, is that our little town took it all in strive, just as we took the devastating floods of 85 and 95. Like we took the closing of our local high school to consolidation and like we even took the loss of the Football Championship in 1952! My wife will likely never again see her pretty face on the BBC, but she says she'll live without it, she guesses.

The consensus in our town is that the Government didn't have much to do when they spent over $65,000,000.00, (so I hear), to convict Ms. Stewart of whatever it was they convicted her of. Frankly, I did not realize it was illegal to lie to the FBI, unless of course, one was under oath! But them I'm not a lawyer, but it seems a lot of people lie and get away with it! The increase in

Overtime costs to the already short-handed prison was probably taken care of by the Fiscal end of the Department of Justice, but the little odds and ends, I'm sure, added up to a sizable chunk of change out of your pocket and mine.

The truth of the matter is that Alderson probably profited by Martha's stay. The Limousine driver her mother and her daughter asked for each week, when they came to visit, (a local lay-leader in the Methodist Church), said they always managed to allow him the chance to go to services on Sunday when they had engaged him. The local Hospitality House, which as their particular mission, provides free accommodations to the often poor relatives of the women in prison, received without having been asked,, after a visit and a Thanksgiving Day meal by Martha's mother, a plethora of badly needed bed linens, curtains and bath towels from the Martha Stewart Organization with no fanfare, they just arrived one day, So you see, while I have laughed and retold with gusto the many Martha Stewart jokes, and I have forwarded on to my friends the many cartoons of Martha in Prison. I think we will have to say that she has handled thus far, the situation with grace and with some semblance of noblesse oblige! She may have gained that grace and understanding of her responsibilities to the less fortunate, the forgotten, the prisoners, both real and only in their own minds, among us. Perhaps we can all learn a little from Ms. Martha

Great Flood of 1985 And Miss Edith

John McCurdy 04

The Great Flood of 1985 caused much devastation in Alderson. the flood did not affect my family directly, we were inconvenienced by the shortage of water while the Water Treatment Plant was being cleaned up, by traffic of gawkers coming to see the damage, but living on the hill overlooking the community we were much luckier than many.

We felt we must help as much as we could, my wife, Pearl, spent hours at the one Church in town that had not been flooded preparing and serving meals to persons who had been flooded and to the many volunteers who had rushed to the area to assist the community in its recovery. I recall that in the two weeks following the flood my wife and I managed to set down to only one meal together.

The Mayor of the town had asked me to organize and be in charge of the Flood Relief efforts in the community and one of the things I did was visit every home in the flood zone and try to assess the most immediate needs of the household. The smell of the flood waters, the odor of spilled fuel oil and washed out septic tanks combined with the hopelessness on many peoples faces, some who had very little before the flood and now had lost even that, will stay with me for a long time! But it afforded me the chance to meet one of the most delightful of all people

****

Miss Edith Berkley and her bachelor brother Everette owned and lived in what we inAlderson, still call the Lobban House, a Victorian era house; it was in less than pristine condition. Brother Everette was a very bright, likeable and eccentric individual who knew a lot about everything. but Miss Edith and I bonded immediately, a delightful spinster lady of unknown age, she was interested in everything on Gods Green Earth. She had scrapbooks galore, packed with clippings on every subject, pasted into inexpensive lined note-books. The several other times I visited, for my own pleasure, we talked of everything. She would begin one story, suddenly think of something else and change to that, I loved it!

We talked of things I only barely remembered from farm life in the 30's and 40's, , old time foods and recipes, things I remembered only faint bits and pieces of from my childhood. I asked her if she remembered what I called, "head cheese or liver pudding", "oh goodness do I"? she exclaimed , "do you like it"? When I said I loved it only a little less than I loved life itself, we were friends and kindred spirits for life!

A man has promised me 3 or 4 hog heads, when I get them, I'll make you some", she said. Now for the city-dwellers and other panty-waists in the audience, "pudding or cheese" is made from the head, liver, and other best not mentioned portions of the hog, along with onions, cornmeal and perhaps other ingredients. It is, at the best, about 150% pure cholesterol and 50% pure lard. It is also indescribably delicious! With two fried eggs, grits and biscuits with country butter and some home-made grape jelly one would cheerfully go to ones Maker after such a meal, (and one just might, surely one's life might be shortened a bit, but it might be well worth it)!

We sat and talked in her kitchen, brother Everette was in his rocker in his corner, working on his corns and trimming his toenails, the two hound dogs were lying by the woodstove which had overflowing ashes to the point I feared a fire, the cat was on the kitchen table and all was right with the world.

A few weeks passed, Miss Edith called from a neighbors house to tell me to come by, in her kitchen she took a pan of pudding from the refrigerator and with a paring knife rapidly carved an orange and an apple and placed them on the pudding and with a flourish and a practiced hand covered the pan with a plastic wrap! When my wife saw it she exclaimed," Miss Edith did that"?

After several days, of lusting to fry it up, and remembering the cat on the table, and Everette working on his toenails and I would decide to wait for another day. Finally, to my everlasting shame, I gave it to the birds. I saw Miss Edith sometime in the next few days and I lied like a dog to my shame. I hope she forgives me.

"Moochie" Tyler

John McCurdy 04

After his business days in Alderson were over, Bill "Moochie" Tyler moved to Pence Springs, He operated a tavern across the road from the "Riverside Inn that Ashby Berkley made into a well known "gourmet " eatery.

On a Saturday night in 1948, Jim Cook, Wally Callahan, Bill Bryant and I had gone to Hinton to see Pat Shires play football. We were in Jim's car, (Jim's dad was Fleet Cook who managed the local CJ's store and they almost always had a new car)! After the post game activities while on the way back to Alderson, we decided to stop in Moochies, someone in the car wanted cigarettes or perhaps we thought there was a chance Mooch would sell us some beer.

He would not, even though the place was as empty as my pockets. So we politely thanked him and started to leave. There was a large cast-iron stove in the middle of the room, the stove-pipe ran up and then horizontally, suspended by wires hung from the ceiling, across the room and into a chimney at the far end.

Now we are talking about four finely honed athletes, agile and graceful and quick as a mongoose, also maybe just a little tiddly, (as my Aunt Mim used to say! One of us, and I really never knew which one, apparently kicked a leg or a brick, which must have been precariously balancing the stove. The stove fell on its side and every damn joint of the stove-pipe came apart and fell to the floor scattering black soot everywhere!

We were completely at a loss, we didn't know what to do, but digging deep into out jeans we came up with about $13.00 which we gave to Mr. Tyler, as he was now known to us, with our heartfelt apology, Mr. Tyler surveyed the damage, took the money from our eager hands, and then reached into his pocket and pulled out the biggest revolver I had ever seen. We were heading for the door, when he said, "thanks for the money boys, but that won't feed the Bulldog"!

Later, dirty beyond belief, covered with soot, tired as coolies, sitting on the edge of the car seats on blankets from the trunk but finally headed up the road toward safety and Alderson at last, I can remember Jimmy Cook plaintively saying, "Did y'all see any Bulldog? I didn't see any damn Bulldog; I don't think he even had one"!

Most Romantic Moments

John MCCurdy 04

In late summer in 1957, my wife and I and our young son had spent the weekend with friends in Front Royal. After a weekend of too much laughter and too much food, we reluctantly said good-bye and prepared to for the drive back to my parents home between Rockbridge Baths and Kerr's Creek.

On a whim at the last minute we decided we would travel back to Lexington by the Skyline Drive. It was early on the Mid-September evening when we drove onto that beautiful, (but slow), highway. Warm, as September nights can be, and peaceful, as the Virginia mountains are when one has been away, we slowly made our way along the mountain top toward Rockbridge County.

We had, that spring, bought a new Ford Convertible, and the top was down at every opportunity. As the night became late the moon came out and the evening fogs began to roll into the valley below. Our son was safely sleeping in the back seat, there was great music everywhere one tuned the radio. There was almost no other traffic sharing our road, and at 40 miles an hour driving was not difficult.

Below us the Valleys of Virginia filled with fog, wisps of mist drifted across the road and off in the distance in the moonlight the crests of the mountains stood like islands in the fog. My dear wife slid to the middle of the seat and leaned her head onto my shoulder as sweethearts sometimes do, and as sweethearts sometimes I put my arm around her shoulder and drew her near.

Life was good, we were young and we would live forever, and I wished that night would never end.

I still have the wife, I still have the son, I still come to family in the county, and we still occasionally drive those mountaintops. The convertible is gone, as is the youth, but the memory of that night is mine (ours) to share forever.

Lynette "Squeaky" Fromme

FRW Memories 6

By John McCurdy '04

Lynette Fromme was in most ways one could think of a very likeable individual. She was perverted in her worship of Charles Manson and, as far as I am concerned, in her view of the American social system. My wife, Pearl, was the Admissions Officer at Alderson when Lynette was first admitted to the prison here.

She did not find Lynette to be very cooperative on her arrival, but we later decided this was likely due to her misconceptions of the world she was about to enter. First impressions are lasting however, and my wife never grew to regard Lynette in a very favorable way.

As a Supervisor, I was well aware that I was regarded by the inmates as having much more power than I actually did, but I was a man, and as a man I was to be manipulated as they had manipulated men in their past. I also was a manipulator as are all correctional workers and it "took one to know one", and I was better at it than they were!

Lynette was housed in the Maximum Security Unit as the result of various sorts of unacceptable behavior, and she had minimal contacts with other inmates. She was allowed to have a little garden spot behind the unit and she spent her time allowed for recreation in the garden, plucking insects from the flower plants and cultivating her little piece of the Earth. One may recall, in her public comments, following her attempt to take President Gerald Ford's life, she made many long, rambling statements about the damage we were doing to the environment.

In someway she learned that I gardened and I thus became her resource person in agriculture; periodically she would send word to me that things were not well in her garden. I would try to go see what the problems were as soon as I could. I recall that in one instance, her two tomato plants had been almost eaten up by an invading force of Flea Beetles. In answer to her query about a remedy, I, like a smart aleck, told her I generally shot them! She didn't contact me for several weeks after that!

Over the next several years, I became her unofficial counselor, and we became friends as much as was possible under the circumstances. I know I developed a liking for her, and we would often talk about many things neither of us knew very much about.

That fall I was on assignment that rarely allowed me the time to get to visit with either Lynette of her fellow Manson follower Sandra Goode. In December I decided to retire and do other things with my life. I regret I did not go tell them goodbye.

About a month after retirement I received a very poignant later from them taking me to task for not having done just that. In it they expressed their thanks for my time and assistance and for my friendship to them. Both Pearl and I were very touched by, what we felt, was the sincerity of the letter.

In the envelope they had enclosed some seeds that they said were of a special flower. I did not plant them. I just was not that sure!

Surviving

John C. McCurdy

2003

So let's see if we can figure out how the hell I survived!

Testing the ice on the creek all by my lonesome and finding out the hard way that it was too thin.

Swimming, with Bob and "Chuuie" Adkins, the Ohio River near Pomeroy, pushing the blackberries we had picked ahead of us on a board to sell for Movie money!

Almost being drowned, when a paddle-wheeler appeared suddenly and swamped me. Being aided by 'Chuukie".

Letting Sonny Fitzpatrick shoot pop bottles out of my hand with his .22 rifle.

Jumping from the hay mow with no idea of what lay below in

Swimming in Kerr's Creek alone

Swimming in Kerr's Creek in flood

Swimming in Kerr's Creeks during Dog Days

Swimming in Kerr's Creek!

Living without Little League to show us how to play ball

Exploring abandoned Coal Mines with a flashlight

Going into Hoys Cave with a flashlight that went out

Getting a .22 rifle on my 12th. Christmas and two boxes of shells

Riding with Leland Feamster at 110 MPH

Riding with Mousie Roach anywhere

Turning over 6 times in Bill Amonette's car with Sugar and Bill,

Catching a freight train at the upper crossing and having to jump off at White Rock

Crawling through the culvert that runs from above the Sid Skaggs house down to the bottom of the hill

Swimming down from Patton's swimming hole to Camp Greenbrier, cutting the dock loose and then swimming down to Markley's

Climbing the water tank,

Jumping off the Alderson bridge in flood waters

Climbing on the long abandoned tipple over a deep shaft mine with water below, falling in and again being saved by "Chuukie" Adkins

Climbing in the Window at the VMI Pool and swimming alone

Surviving the chewing out I received from Herb Patchin once when he caught me

Tubing in Goshen Pass, every summer there were drowning in that very stream!

Walking the railing on the Memorial Bridge over to the W&L Athletic Fields with Woods Creek 100 feet below

Riding double on Ronnie Jordan's "Whizzer Motor Bike" over all of Rockbridge County

Hitch hiking

The polio years that so many of my age didn't survive

The thrashings I got with a Japonica branch from my Mom

The coldness of my Dad when he disapproved

Four years making Nitroglycerine

27 years working with convicts

Being a parent

The loss of so many valuable people from my life

The terrible lonely feeling one has when they realize there is no one left to ask,.

The Attorney General's Flag

FRW Memories 7

John McCurdy   05

At the FRW there were always inmates whose age, health or other good reasons kept from being required to work a full day or in some cases to work at all. Since the beginnings of the institution these people were always taken care of in a way that met their needs, as well as the needs of the institution.

Many of the women were from the bigger cities like NYC, and many of them were skilled in the arts needed in the clothing industries of NYC. They were almost always assigned to Dressmaking and Arts. Their talents could be utilized in a way that would benefit both the Institution as a whole and inmates about to be released in particular. The D and A department made release clothing for inmates who did not have the funds or family to provide them with release clothing.

But there was another part of Dressmaking and Arts that had a more delicate and artistic task. The making of the Flag for the Attorney General of the United States. The flag that always, along with the Official U. S. Flag, stood behind the Attorney Generals Desk, in his office in Washington D. C.

That Flag was of white silk and hand-embroidered with the Official Seal of the Office of the Attorney General done in colored silk. The Flag was about five feet long and of a width appropriate, and around the edges were golden tassels also in silk thread! Three or more women often worked for several years in D and A to complete, what was in truth, a Work of Art! When a new Attorney General was appointed, another flag was started!

The Flag was presented to the Attorney General by the Director of the Bureau of Prisons, at a ceremony in the Great Hall of the Department of Justice, and the Attorney General always took his Flag when he left Office!

The Life of the Men at the Woman's Prison

FRW Memories 08
John McCurdy 05

Guys were just sort of tolerated at the Federal Reformatory for Women in the first 50 years of its being. All of the Administrative Staff were women with the occasional man occupying the Business Manager or one of the other slots that requires some profession skill for which no women were readily available. The majority of the Administrators were also single ladies of middle age or older. Most of them had spent their life in the Social Sciences. I was told by a supervisor, "this is a woman's prison, ran by women, has been, always will be."

The prevalent attitude of the FRW to the inmate was paternalistic, close to infantilism. A good indicator of that infantilism would be that the inmate's were called, "girls!" They were expected to refer to themselves as "one of the girls" when they would answer the telephone. The "girls" were not allowed to operate dangerous machinery such as gasoline-powered lawn mowers for fear they would, "hurt themselves"!

The men were used for the most mundane chores, removing screens so that windows could be washed, driving to the Post Office for the mail, bringing it to the Institution Mail Room and dumping it because the lifting would be too much for the woman mail room officer to handle. We were expected to deliver the clean laundry of the officers to the cottages, (making sure we dragged those of the officers we didn't like through a mud-puddle or so)! In addition we were responsible for the security of the institution and for the control of the occasional inmate who acted out. At one time the Male Officers were the "bad guys" who came in, grabbed the inmate, gave her the "bums rush" off to "Davis Hall',   Davis Hall was the building used to handle disciplinary cases and that housed the more dangerous inmates. I soon realized I got much better results with reason than the usual methods., many times the inmates just needed someone to listen to them, a common feeling we all sometime have.

Here might be the place to discuss the question that always seems to come to people's minds. The Sex thing! In all the time I worked at the FRW, about 20 years, I was seriously asked by an inmate only 2 or so times if I were interested in a sexual episode! That is not to say that jokingly extended invitations were not offered that could be just as jokingly declined. At night when patrolling the cottage areas often an anonymous voice would come from a cottage saying, "come on up, big boy," or another remark of some kind, generally followed by the laughter of other women in the cottage. Later when I was a counselor and was involved much more in the intimacy of inmate's lives, it never became a problem. In some cases inmates did develop crushes and several times other inmate would come to me and tell me to be careful around another individual. Until I transferred to another institution in 1975, I had heard of only one instance of an employee/inmate affair! I am dubious about that supposed incident ever occurring!

When I returned to Alderson in 1978 as a supervisor, the institution had changed, men were then assigned as cottage officers and there was much more interaction, just as in men's prisons when women officers began to be assigned to quarters!

Several men and women employees were terminated for fraternization with inmates, and several marriages resulted when the inmate was released. Some of the marriages endured, some didn't! The Bureau of

Prisons was not unaware of what would occur, it was much more of a normal life than what occurs in situations when the opposite sex is not present. One should remember that seduction took place between inmate/staff even in same sex situations! Love or Lust can't really be very well regulated, and that's probably a good thing!

The Christmas Elf on the Coffee table

By John McCurdy, '03

In the Early 50's Beulah Rigg gave me a little ceramic Red Elf; conical hat, pointy-toed shoes and all. It was at some Church function that she gave it to me, probably as a joke. It sat on the mantle that Christmas and then was put away with all the other decorations and baubles of our Christmas. The following Yule Time it came out of hiding to resume a spot somewhere in our home as a decoration.

It was on the third year that my wife, Pearl, asked it I would make for her a small pine log with two holes bored in the top for candles. I had just cut several feet from the bottom of our Christmas tree, so finding the material was not hard to do. I drilled two holes in the middle of the "log", but she did not want them in the middle of the wood. That was easy to fix, I cut about 8 inches from one end and it was, in her words, "just perfect".

She put two red candles and some fresh greenery along with a few magnolia leaves I had swiped from the tree in L. O. McClung's yard, and then she spied the Little Red Elf. When she placed him on the log amid the greenery, the small scene was complete.

For over 50 years now the Little Red Elf has stood faithful watch over the Christmases of our family. The greenery are renewed each year, the candle drippings have accumulated in the rough bark , and the dings and the dents have become more noticeable each year on it, as they have on us. Like us with each other, and like the memories shared, the Little Red Elf on the Coffee Table becomes more precious each year. Each year we remember "Bute" Rigg and we retell the tale of the "Little Red Elf".

I often wonder if that is not what Immortality is all about.

The Prison Riots

FRW Memories 9

John McCurdy, "05

In 1970 the Alderson Prison experienced the first riot in its fifty year history. The permissive atmosphere of the 60's and 70's had led the FRW and, indeed, many prisons through-out the country to experiment with new and unproven theories of rehabilitation, incarceration and inmate freedom. Alderson was no different! A permissive program, whether in the home or elsewhere, is the easiest way; until the time comes when one has to become a little bit more controlling, then the difficulties begin with resistance ranging from foot-dragging to complete rebellion.

You recall, I'm sure, the Attica Riot in New York State. It has been dissected by the amateurs and the professionals ad nauseam with no answers yet found. The FRW was in a permissive mode also. When a group of inmates, mostly black, came to Warden Virginia McLaughlin and wanted permission to hold a memorial service outdoors for the INMATES who were killed in that riot, she permitted the service to be held.

When rain began to fall early that cool evening, the leaders of the vigil asked the Warden if they could go into the recently vacated building that had in the past housed the Garment Factory. The warden again said yes, (the second mistake)! Without any restraints from the Executive Staff the situation soon deteriorated into a crisis, the inmates, in small groups, soon left the Old Garment Factory, went to their Cottages and returned with blankets, mattresses and food-stuffs to sustain themselves. Over the next several days, while several abortive attempts were made resolve the situation, in the absence of effective leadership from the Executive Staff, nothing was accomplished! After much too long a time the Bureau was informed that the situation was out of hand and that this institution was not able to resolve it! That night the Riot-Control Teams from several nearby Federal Prisons began to arrive, including Ashland, Kentucky; Petersburg, Virginia and the Youth Center at Morgantown, West Virginia. My younger brother Lee was a member of the Petersburg Riot-Control Squad.

The Executive Staff at Alderson had little experience in dealing with situations like the one they faced. They did not realize that quick, decisive action was needed until it was much too late. The Warden, purportedly, asked the Petersburg and Ashland Control Teams to not wear their protective gear of helmets, face-masks, gloves, vests and above all, not to carry their batons. They were asked to go into the building and bring the inmates out. One of the team's members reportedly asked her if she had taken leave of her senses! It was shortly after this that the Warden was relieved of duty by Mason Holley of the Central Office of the Bureau of Prisons. She returned after the situation was resolved.

Two officers had been assigned to each cottage shortly after the problem became apparent to supervise the inmates who had not joined in the riot.

On day three and after the Lewisburg Penitentiary Control Team arrived the action leading to the end of the Riot was commenced.

Two Alderson officers and one man from the Riot Control Team of Lewisburg Penitentiary were assigned to each cottage. The next morning the Prison Buses drove up to the cottages and as the inmates involved in the riot were identified by Alderson Staff, they were loaded into the buses!

Other inmates not yet in the Riot Control Teams custody, began to break window in the cottages and inflict as much damage as they could on the furnishings in the cottage, they also began to go into cottages other than their own and hide. After calling for all inmates to vacate the cottages, CS gas was introduced into them and the remainder of the inmates came out.

On a personal note; Melvin Huffman, who was assigned to photograph the operation took a photograph of me shaking my finger under the nose of an inmate who wanted to get on the bus in sympathy with someone. At the front of the bus was my Brother Lee in full riot gear putting someone on the bus. Standing at the front of the bus with Pat Bennett was my wife Pearl, they were putting on gas-masks preparatory to going into a gassed cottage to insure that no inmate were in there overcome and unable to leave. I was unable to secure a copy of that photo. I would love to have been able give it to my Mother and ask her if she knew what her kids were up to!

The women who had participated in the riots and who were on the busses were taken to the Cabell County Jail in Huntington, West Virginia until a wing of a Cell-house at the FCI in Ashland, Kentucky could be made ready for them. Reportedly they trashed the Huntington Jail. Ashland, in turn, got rid of them as soon as possible!

In the weeks following the riots, Administrative Hearings were held, and many inmates who had not been transferred in the busses at the conclusion of the riot, were afforded hearings to determine whether or not they had been a participant. I was asked to be the Staff Representative for several women,   all of whom swore to me on their Mothers Graves that they had not been a part in any thing bad, EVER! I especially remember a girl named Dorothy who was on my caseload and was accused of assaulting a staff member in a disturbance on the Upper Campus. When we entered the Hearing Room I asked her if she knew everyone there. Sitting in the chair next to the chair I had pointed out for her, was Eddie Lightner, Eddie had a pained look on his face and when Dorothy saw him, she said, " Hell John, let's get out of here"! It was Eddie she had kicked in the crotch, apparently quite hard from the look on his face! Dorothy went to California, but she did return to Alderson in a few years. I never failed to tell her if I had run into Eddie, even if I had just made it up!

My wife Pearl was on duty over 24 hours at a time once or twice during this time and I worked 44 hours without getting home, catching cat-naps as time was available, other people worked harder and longer. It is my opinion that most of the Alderson Staff acted very admirably in the situation.

The FRW learned valuable lessons in this affair. The Bureau insisted that Riot Control Teams receive more training and adequate equipment within the institution and that the procedures and tables of organization needed to be more clearly defined in the event of another disturbance. A Training Officer with experience in men's institutions was brought in to develop the programs for some of the things that were needed!

In 1973-4 Alderson had another uprising that needed other institutions help, but this time the FRW was better prepared and was able to participate in the action. I am unaware of any other disturbances on anything other than a very small scale having occurred since then.

Punch Jones and his Rock

John McCurdy'03

In the spring of 1928, Punch was pitching horseshoes with his daddy in a vacant lot near their home in Peterstown, West Virginia. Sixteen years later he was killed in action near the Rhine River in Germany!

On this happier day his horseshoe dislodged an object, odd-shaped, about three- quarters of an inch in diameter. Punch put it in his pocket, and later, before going into the house, he put it on the front porch behind one of the posts. His mother, finally tiring of sweeping around it, and after having swept it off the porch a few times, moved it to a window ledge. Every now and then, Punch would show the neighborhood kids his "diamond", as he called it.

Many years later one of the Jones kids attended VPI and took a Geology course, he learned about the "scratch test' of mineral and crystals. When he was at home he tried Punch's rock; it scratched everything he tried! When the stone was taken to Dr. Roy Holden of the Geology Department at Virginia Polytechnic Institute, it was pronounced, after testing, that the stone, indeed, was a diamond! Not just a diamond, but one of good color and relatively free of imperfections! The 34.5 alluvial, (brought by glaciers), diamond was the largest ever found in the United States!

It was loaned to the Smithsonian Institution and remained there a number of years. Punch Jones, the finder of the stone, had grown up, gotten married, gone to war, and lost his life.

Pretty much by general agreement the stone was considered the joint property of William "Punch" Jones and his father Grover Cleveland Jones. Upon the death of Punch, his share, of course was his wife's, she subsequently sold her share to one of Punch's brothers, who also acquired his fathers share of the stone.

Sometime later, the diamond, still referred to as, "the Punch Jones Diamond," was reclaimed from the Smithsonian and embarked on the rounds of fairs and expositions. A small, home-built trailer about five by eight feet became its exhibition hall. At the West Virginia State Fair in the 90's one could, for a few dollars, gaze at the wonderful stone, reposing on a black cushion, encased in glass, safe behind a rope protecting it from prying hands.

I am unsure of the whereabouts of the Punch Jones diamond today, my guess that it is safe somewhere, lying on a black pillow, I'm sure it's not on a window sill !

The Rolls Royce

More From Kerr's Creek

John McCurdy 05

Mr. Billie, of W. E. Fitzpatrick and Sons General Store, just where US Route 60 goes over Kerr's Creek east of Lexington , Virginia; decided in the summer of 1946 that it would be a good idea to open the long closed little brick Esso gas station, located beside his general store. The general store sold Gulf gasoline products, so with the opening of the adjacent Esso station Mr. Billie would just about have a lock on the gas business. The War was just over and rationing was a thing of the past, tires and other things were becoming readily available once more, and automobile traffic on Route 60 seemed to increase every day.

I was Mr. Fitzpatrick's neighbor and his sometimes right-hand man in the store-clerking business. I was the boy who was just the right man to run the new business venture. Each morning as close to 8 o'clock as I could make it, (15-16 year old boys are not the most punctual of people), I would be given twenty dollars in currency and a few dollars in coins and I would open the Esso station for the business of the day.

The station, which still stands, was one room with a portico built on the front to shelter folks from inclement weather, a ladies and a men's rest-room in each rear corner with outside entrances and with running water! There were two grades of gasoline, High-Test and Regular with large glass containers on top that had to be filled with a lever- action pump before any gasoline could be dispensed.

The station had a soda cooler with a sliding top, with cold bottles of Coca-Cola, Orange Crush, Grapette (at only 6 ounces a bottle only wealthy folks or show-offs bought that), and of course, R.C. Cola at a full 12 ounces to the bottle. An R.C. and a bag of salted peanuts for one to put in it was a young lad's favorite!

There was a bench just outside the front entry and I spent a large part of the day sitting on it watching the cars and truck zip right on past. Occasionally I would get so exhausted I would have to go inside and stretch out on the counter using a coil-spring seat pad for a pillow. The counter was just the right length, a three-foot case that held candies and chewing gum and other sundries took up the rest of the counter.

The screech of tires and the blowing of horns aroused me, in front of my place of employment were a big touring car and a Greyhound Bus, The bus was sitting on the highway and the driver had the door open and was demanding that the driver of the car explain why he had pulled into the service station without warning, with no signal or anything, he was mad! The driver of the car was having trouble with an explanation. He did not speak the most distinct version of the American brand of the English language and between that and the bus-driver not giving him much chance, he was not doing a very good job of getting his explanation understood by the other driver!

By that time, of course, I was in the middle of the furor. I was able to make out from the cars driver that he had indeed signaled! The difficulty was in the fact that the Bus Driver could not see the signal because the top was up on the touring car and the car was one with right-hand drive! Not only was it right-hand drive but it was a Rolls-Royce! Finally the fuss abated the two drivers shook hands and all was well.

We, the driver and I, fueled his car and checked the oil on the magnificent engine.

Two spark plugs for each cylinder, a distributor and a magneto ignition, redundancy to assure that if one element failed it would not inconvenience the driver The driver explained that he was from the Netherlands, was visiting the USA, had purchased the Rolls for $500.00 in New York City and planned to drive it to the west coast, sell the car and return to NYC and then to Holland. He drank two Grapettes, so we know he was rich; ate a candy bar and some bread and cheese he had in his car, visited the rest-room, and then after I helped him lower the top on his automobile and having me write my name and address in a journal he was keeping he drove off on his great adventure.

About a year later I had a note from him that he had written from the Netherlands telling me he'd made it!

In the years since, when I have driven west, I never fail to think of the tragedy averted one sleepy day on Kerr's Creek, and wonder what my young Dutch friend did with the rest of his life.

The Skater

John McCurdy 05

Kerr's Creek in the winter time and in the wartime years of 1941 to 1945 was a hard place for a poor kid to find much in the way of leisure time's activities and amusements, not many of us considered chipping ice from watering troughs or carrying slop to the hogs to be amusement. Participation in high school sports or other activities was difficult because of the weather and chores and the shortness of the winter day. The coming of the "Activities Bus" was an idea far in the future.

It was a rare country boy who had access to a automobile other than on very rare and specials occasions, television was as far in the future as the "Activities Bus"! Only Harrisonburg and a Roanoke station were available until nightfall on our old Stromberg- Carlson Table model radio, and then our parents insisted on deciding what station we were going to listen too, after Gabriel Heatter, the rest of their choices left us pretty much hung out to dry, and they didn't care a bit! Homework wasn't an especially attractive alternative except for a few kids, even though all of our parents thought it was a great idea!

When the McCown boys announced that the ice in the creek behind their house was frozen to the bottom and there was going to be a skating party and everyone was invited, there was much anticipation in the community. Kids were home from the services and from college; it was the Christmas season and excitement was in the air. It was possibly the first such community event in several years.

Most of the ice-skates in the community had not been used or even seen for many years and when finally found, most of them were covered with a layer of rust. They were the type of skate than clamped onto the soles of ones shoes, and, of course the special wrench, called a "skate key' used to tighten the skate clamp onto the shoe soles was also missing. Many parents did not like the skates because, because according to them, "they ruined shoes". None the less, skates were cleaned of rust, they were oiled and some method of tightening them was improvised. We were fast getting ready for the big night!

I don't remember having asked for them but the previous Christmas I had gotten a pair of black leather shoe skates. ($7.50 from Montgomery Wards.) There had not been a freeze since then, as you might know! I was determined to go to the party which was about three miles west of our house on Route 60. Now in those days parents didn't provide transportation to such unimportant things as recreation for their kids, getting there, in their eyes, was "part of the recreation". Just a little whining on my part convinced me my parents weren't going to take me; there was even a suggestion that at the age of 13 going on 14, I didn't have any business being at the party in the first place!

I knew that my gorgeous neighbor, the very sweet Margorie Fitzpatrick was sure to be going and that she was a sucker for poor kids with sad stories. I promptly made a trip to her house to ask if I could go to the party with her and her date. She readily agreed and her date, young Mason Deaver, Jr. tried very hard to act as though I was welcome!

The party was all one could have hoped for, I'm sure I was among the youngest there, but my skates fit, and I was actually able to stand and move a few steps. Refreshments were served and Mrs. McCown and her husband even took a turn around the ice.

The high point of the evening was just about to begin:

"Red" Sicily was a young First Lieutenant assigned to the School for Special Services at Washington and Lee University. Among his many talents he was a skater! A professional, he had at one time been a member of the Sonja Henie skating troupe. A friend of several people at the party, it was at their invitation he had attended. It was obvious the minute he stepped onto the frozen creek, that he was special, even simply skating around his grace on ice was apparent.

After much cajoling from the group, he took the ice alone. He did all the things I had dreamed of being able to do. He glided and skated on first one leg and then on the other, he skated backwards and forwards and even sideways. He flew   and   he soared   and

The rough, rough, uneven ice of our Kerr's Creeks became, for a moment, the Ice Rink at Madison Square Garden or Rockefeller Center. And we for that moment were part of something that comes very seldom.

All else was anticlimactic. I was in a daze. I remember Mason Deaver letting me out of his Pontiac and saying, "your domicile, young Sir". Which I thought was pretty sophisticated and awfully nice of him, since I was an interloper in the car in the first place!

Margorie Fitzpatrick, of course, later married "Red" Sicily. They built a home on a hilltop on Kerr's Creek, living there until "Red' died at much too early an age.

The Veteran

(Old Man Dixon)

John McCurdy '04

"Them Pipes and Some Black Maria Plug," after sixty years I can still hear his guttural

hard-to-understand voice as he pointed to a card of corncob pipes, (a card contained a dozen pipes, attached with a little metal clip to the cardboard). Black Maria was the chewing tobacco equivalent of cigar butts and black-strap molasses. It was a MAN'S chew!

Each month after Mr. Deaver, the rural postal mail carrier, had delivered his government pension check to his mail box, Mr. Dixon would get his old feed sack and walk to the J. D. Fitzpatrick and Sons General Store on Kerr's Creek near Lexington, Virginia. Mr. Billy, the stores owner and operator would have conveniently had to go next door to his house when Mr. Dixon hit the door leaving me, his 15 year old part-time and Saturdays and fulltime in the summer clerk, in charge of the whole she-bang, especially the waiting on of Mr. Dixon.

There is no one left today to tell me much about Mr. Dixon, not even his first name, he lived in a small cabin on the bank of "Big Springs" the site of a raid and massacre by an Indian War-Party led by Cornstalk. The massacre that in turn, led to the death of

Cornstalk in Point Pleasant! The cabin is long gone; it likely dated to about the time of the Raid. I thought at the time that Mr. Dixon was a relative of the Wash family that lived in a large manor house nearby, and who owned part of the "Big Spring", apparently he was not!

Each month he would walk the mile or so to the store on Old Route 60 with his sack in which to carry home his supplies. He had little to say to a kid or to anyone else. I had heard that he had been gassed in France in the World War and that his throat and his lungs and vocal cords had been blistered by the gas that afterwards speaking was very difficult. I remember that Mr. Fitzpatrick always spoke very kindly of him even though he didn't want to wait on him. I wondered why. Mr. Billy had also been in France but never talked about it. I now wonder if that was why he preferred to be gone when Mr. Dixon came to the store. If perhaps it reminded him of things he would prefer not remembering!

I'm sure he bought more supplies than just pipes and tobacco, and when he had finished his shopping he would go on the Stores Porch and sit on one of the benches there. He would slice slivers of Black Maria into one of the new pipes and after using several kitchen matches and doing a lot of sucking on the pipe, finally get it lit. He would draw the smoke deep into his lungs; it must have been incredibly hot and strong. He'd sit awhile and watch the traffic on Route 60, nod to folks coming into the store, watch me pumping gas and then shoulder his sack and leave. When I asked Mr. Billy about the pipes and tobacco, he said, "That's the only way he can taste it"! I think that was the first inking I had of what wars were really about!

Wire Grimmett

By John McCurdy

In the 60's Bobby Withrow and Phyllis came back from Germany on their annual visit home. Bob was assigned to the State Department at the Spandau Prison where the German war criminals were housed.

Having diplomatic immunity their luggage was not subject to inspection upon entering the country. Like any prudent Alderson boy would have done, Bobby had his luggage packed with good booze from the duty free commissaries and PX's of the Allies in Berlin. To make a long story more interesting, in the course of a short night followed by a long and sick day, Withrow and I decided that the career move I needed to make was to transfer from the Federal Prison Service to the State Department and Spandau. The next day when I had recovered it still seemed like a good idea, unlike many of our ideas cooked up under similar circumstances!

I applied for the transfer and the story immediately made the rounds of Alderson that it was a done deal. A few days afterward I had a telephone call from "Wire" Grimmett", one of the local "beer-joints better customers," asking if he could talk to me in a few hours. Mystified, I told him he would be welcome.

About six o'clock, Wire appeared, in a suit and tie and sober and clean shaven as a regular citizen. Invited in, he preferred the back porch. After a minute of small talk, he got down to business. He said he had been told I was transferring to Berlin, Germany; and that to get to Berlin I would have to pass through the Russian controlled Sector of Germany: then he began his story.

As a GI during the advance into Germany, during which time they had gotten far ahead of their supporting forces, Wire said he had came into possession of something of immense value, although he was very vague about how he had gained that possession. In the next day or so, he was severely wounded and was then   inadvertently left behind by his fellow GIs. After spending a night alone, he realized he was not likely to die from his wounds,   but he was unable to walk.   He knew that no matter who got to him first, either counter-attacking German troops or rescuing GIs, he was likely to lose his treasure and perhaps his life!

He determined that he was in the southeast corner of an apple orchard located near a large stone church, and that the corner of a stone wall that he was near would likely survive the conflict it has thus far endured. With his bayonet he dug a foot-deep hole in the corner of the wall and in it he buried what he described as a leather pouch containing many cut diamonds! He hoped that if rescued, or even if captured, he might one day be able to return and retrieve his lost treasure.

Rescued by advancing American troops, taken to the hospital in the rear and then back to the US, he was never able to secure the funds to pay for his trip back to Germany.

His proposal to me was that I stop along the highway to Berlin, climb the chain-link fence that was now in place along the highways entire length and retrieve the long-lost pouch from the corner of the wall. There were a number of reasons I didn't think this was a very good idea.

I knew the Russian Military patrolled the higway both be motor vehicle and from the air and

that traffic was timed from one end to the other, two good reasons for one not to be stopping to climb fences. In addition, I would have been flown into Berlin and not have been anywhere close to the lost jewels. With regret, I declined Wire's request.

In the years since then, and at Wire's funeral, I wondered if his problematic life after service was partly a result of his "lost fortune" and "what might have been"!

Several years later I flew into and out of Berlin the same day, I thought of Wires dilemma with sadness for him.

A Prison Christmas in Alderson

FRW Memories 10

John McCurdy 04

The most joyous time of the year was the saddest time of the year in the Federal prison for women at Alderson. Being away from their children, their families and other loved ones was a pretty rotten way to spent Christmas.

The staff at the prison was always well aware of the difficulty and heartaches being endured by the inmates at this time of year and as a result there was an unspoken agreement that we would do what we could to make the season a little more bearable. We just didn't see every infraction of the rules, disrespectful behavior was sometimes ignored, and rules were often bent if not broken for a few days in December.

All of us hated to work on the Holidays, we were away from our own families but we knew that in a few hours we would be home around the family fires. Somehow home made candies and cookies appeared in the cottages and on the work details of the inmates. Christmas decorative items that were obviously not Government Issue mysteriously appeared on the hall tables. Extra strings of lights decorated the doors and no supervisor would have asked where they came from for fear they might have came from their own houses.

Tempers would flare and nasty words would erupt followed by tears and avowals of "forgive me; you know I didn't mean that".

128

Handmade gifts would be exchanged between inmates and if the truth were told between some staff and inmates; for in many cases a staff member was the only person an inmate had that she could love and the love was often returned, for the staffs own family were sometimes scattered and the inmates became the family.

The cottages were decorated with items stored in the attics from year to years, with handmade decorations filched from various workplaces, toilet paper snow, paper cup bells and tin can bottoms made into stars.

A yearly competition was held to see which cottage would have the most original and best decorations, judged by retired staff who welcomed the opportunity to again be a part of the Christmas festivity and to perhaps renew acquaintances with some of the inmates, some of the cottages had skits they would produce for the judges, and the decision as to the winners was always greeted with somewhat good-natured complaints by the losers.

There were always some old-timers and lifers who had watched staff kids grow into adulthood and who had adopted, in a way, those kids as their own. Christmas was the time to bring them up-to-date with what was happening with their/our children. Many tears were shared at these poignant times.

Now is not the time to tell about the home-made raisin-jack, hooch, or other alcohol producing concoctions, but then nobody's perfect, are they?

On The Road to Richlands

John McCurdy

January 05

I only saw it once: or at least, I think I saw it, to tell you the truth, I really hope I didn't! On a lonely stretch of US 60 west of Lewisburg, West Virginia, the site of fine farms that houses the landed gentry of Greenbrier County, a stretch of highway, now traveled only by those living along the roads and by the occasional tourist looking for "local' color. Few know what occurred on this stretch of road on a moonless night in the twenty's. I hope they are never traveling alone on that road, when the fog rolls up from the rivers and creeks and down from the ridges and mountains that surround it.

It is whispered by long-time residents of the area, whispered about only when one is with close friends or dear relatives; that one should not venture on that highway in the times of the fog. Too many strange and unexplainable events have occurred out there then when the fogs roll up from the rivers and down from the hills!

Squire Billings was driving home from Church and lost control of his A-Model Ford and slit his throat on the glass of the windshield of his car. His neighbor Joe Conners was walking along that section of road and was crushed by a falling tree, a giant Elm that had stood there for nearly a hundred years. Joe's brother fell at about the same place and was blinded by a stray strand of barbed wire sticking out from the ground. These are some of the things that were reported in the local paper. Some others were hushed up and the matter taken care of privately by the locals and undertakers and the mental institutions of the day. One would not want to be too awfully inquisitive about the upper rooms of a few of the fine homes along this roadway!

Will Williams was in the Lewisburg Jail, he was accused of molesting a young white woman, it was well known in the community that everyone thereabouts who had desired had also molested her: three or four times if they wished . But she was a white woman, and the safety of all white women in the civilized world was at stake when the mob took Will Williams from the jail and drove out to the Richlands area there to extract their joy and God's retribution on Wills poor black body and his eternal Holy Soul.

He was beaten and tortured and then lynched from a telephone pole along the Roadway, when he resisted dying they lowered him and slit his throat and pulled him up again. Then they built a fire under him and exulted in the aroma of his burnt flesh! When they had finished their bottles and sated their lust for blood they drove away just as the fog rolled over the hills and up from the creeks and obliterated the evil that had been done there.

I'm not sure of what I saw in the fog as I drove that road, but it looked like a man to me!

And I don't want to see anything like that again. I've been told that Will screamed as they put the wire around his neck, "I knows you boys, you know I didn't do nothing wrong, you'll be sorry!

Some one who was there was sorry, every year a envelope with a large amount of money is put in the door of Wesley Methodist Church and a wreath appears on the side of the road near Richlands. But when the fogs roll up from the rivers and creeks and down from the ridges and mountains that surround it, misfortune and tragedy still awaits.

Iva D'Aquino (Tokyo Rose)

FRW memories 11

John McCurdy 06

In the last year I have thought several times about Iva D'Aquino, probably because of the furor in the media about Martha Stewart and her incarceration in Alderson and now after the recent announcement of the death in Chicago of Ive D'Aquino. I won't spend much time on Miss Stewart since I imagine she is still too fresh in your mind, as in mine, to warrant the effort. I think it sufficient to say, that in my opinion, for whatever it's worth. Neither she nor Iva D'Aquino was of sufficient import to warrant the time and money spent on their conviction and subsequent prison time. Both were likely guilty of monumental poor judgment and dumb behavior at times, but who isn't?

Iva Toguri D'Aquino was a victim, a victim of the media, in particular Walter Winchell, who in the 40's was a very powerful radio personality who called himself a reporter. He launched a campaign to have a minor play in the events of 1941-1946. Iva D'Aquino, who was an American citizen visiting the orient, at the beginning of WW2, and who despite her efforts was unable to be repatriated to the USA, branded a traitor.

After the war she had been investigated by the American Forces in Japan and found innocent of any sort of collaboration with the enemy, and was getting ready to return with her husband to the

USA when she came to the attention of Winchell. He launched a vitriolic campaign against her and what he called,"her treason". Harry Truman, who I greatly admire, did a less than admirable thing when he, caving into the pressures of Winchell ordered Attorney General Tom Clark, (incidentally the father of the much less than admired Ramsey Clark, who in my opinion was probably guilty of much more treasonable conduct ! than Ms. D'Aquino), to launch an investigation into the case.

I knew Iva D'Aquino when she was incarcerated in the Federal Reformatory for Women in Alderson. She worked in the prison hospital and during the 3 or 4 years that I knew her, was a lovely person to be around, kind and pleasant to everyone, an opinion shared by most of my co-workers.

I went to the trouble to go to the Records Office and read her file including the Transcript of her trial. That was when I began to have doubts about the validity of the charges that she was accused of committing.

I was on duty the morning of her release from prison, we thought it was a media circus at the time but compared to the craziness of the Martha Stewart case it was a blip in the history of the FRW!

She was released in the early morning hours, her two brothers; short, stout, somber men arrived to pick her up in a black post-war Chrysler and, under heavy escort drove to the Administration Building, where their reunion took place. The prison Record Officer, Iverne Carter rode back to the Front Gate in the car with them. I recall they embraced and Mrs. Carter wished the group a safe journey, Iva rolled the window down and thanked me and said, "God Bless You, Mr. McCurdy". I said the same to her, the car stopped again and the photographers were allowed a few question and then the long black automobile slowly began the trip back to Chicago.

Iva Toguri D'Acquino "Tokyo Rose" was pardoned by President Gerald Ford in 1970. The last I heard, she, as an old woman, was running the store her father had started in Chicago.

Note: Iva D'Aquino died in 2007, her death got mere mention in the national news.

Martha Stewart and Alderson

FRW Memories 12

John McCurdy 05

The thought occurred to me that my old English teacher in Lexington High School, Miss Gertrude Morrison, would really be disappointed in me if I didn't tell you Rockbridge County folks about the thrill of having M's. Martha in our town, well not really in our town, but close, just beyond the Town Limits.

I've been a resident of Alderson for over 50 years now, ever since I left Kerr's Creek and Virginia. Married here and the Federal Bureau of Prisons supported my family in a fairly decent manner. I still however, am proud I was born in Virginia, in Lexington and in the only house General Jackson ever owned!

Well when we realized that Martha was likely to be a guest of our locale, much of the town was a-twitter and when we knew for certain that she was going to be arriving in a few weeks things started happening around here, you can be sure! Betty Alderson of Alderson's Store sent off and had a bunch of T-shirts made that proudly proclaimed "Alderson, a Good Place to Spend Time", right cute, and they sold a zillion, E-Bay and everywhere!

Our little two women, one man Town Hall, was flooded with phone calls and couldn't get the monthly water bills out until

Tommy Roush opened a Media Center, and got a lot of visitors into the Depot Museum that would not normally have visited there, and a lot of strangers that looked vaguely familiar showed up on the streets and the local motel was full and it was not the 4th of July, (Alderson's Big Celebration).

The three restaurants in town were assured of a profitable year with take-outs and the two convenience stores in town sold a bunch of high-priced gasoline!

My wife's Bridge Club, which meets weekly at the Monroe Diner was invaded by big city newspaper folks and network peoples, I think they are called "stringers". Even I was approached while I was picking pole beans in our garden by a columnist from the Hartfort (CT) Courant! I was glad for an excuse to stop and have a glass of iced tea on the porch with him. He promised to send me a copy of the paper, but he didn't'! My wife was even mentioned in People magazine for goodness sake! I talked to them too, but they wanted a woman's point of view, I guess.

While the date of Martha's arrival was known, the exact time and method of arrival was not, so the media didn't take any chances on her slipping in and evading them. As many as a dozen large Satellite TV trucks were parked just off the narrow county road in front of the prisons property half in and half out of the ditch. The television commentators were extremely well dressed from the waist up, but they were a muddy mess from there down! An adjacent landowner was charging, and getting, $750.00 a week for a parking place! He probably was the only person who was sorry to see the folks go. News photographers with big lens cameras were skulking everywhere around the prison grounds perimeter taking photos of the grounds and the cottages for background stories, and just for something to do probably.

Martha fooled everyone by flying into Beckley by charter aircraft and then being brought the 50 miles to Alderson by a Beckley security service. She did not stop for an interview.

In talking with folks now employed at the prison, it seems that they don't think its anything special, it's another day's work. If "Squeaky" Fromme, Axis Sally and Tokyo Rose could take it, good old Martha Stewart can take it also! If she can stand us, we can stand her, and that seems to be the feelings around here!

I thought you might like a record of a local boy who was a witness to history!

Pat Robertson

John McCurdy 04

One of the not especially memorable schoolmates of my in high school years in Lexington, Virginia, was Pat Robertson, yes, I'm telling you, it was the very same Pat Robertson!

It was the understanding of the students in LHS that Pat had been kicked out of some rather prestigious prep school, probably "up north", and for some unknown reason. We were soon made to know that he would not be our schoolmate long, only until the end of the current semester.

Pat's dad was, of course, A. Willis Robertson; the junior United Stated Senator from the State of Virginia. The colleague of the long-time senior Senator from out state, the well-known Harry Byrd, (no relation to West Virginia's renowned fiddle-player Robert Byrd).

Daddy Robertson resembled the son, or perhaps the son resembles the father would be more accurate; the florid complexion, the long white hair, the pompous attitude, and above all the ability to speak, as someone once said of Hubert Humphrey, "about any subject, whether or not he knew anything about it" He, in the several times I was at their home for some reason; certainly not as a social equal, had the ability to speak to me of my Father and my Mother, and indeed of little old me, as though he were an intimate friend of long years to my family. Only after thinking over what he had had to say would I realize he had never once uttered my name. It was for a good reason, he didn't know it! But some day I would be of voting age and therefore I was to be cultivated.

Pat was not a friend, I don't remember him having any friends, he had spent little time of his life in Lexington, and I'm sure just did not know many kids. A pudgy big kid, he hung around, as I recall, with the daughter of one of the local physicians. He did not engage in any sports and when I go back to the year books of those days he is not pictured or named in any class or in any activity! Looking back on those days, he was there but he was absent!

At the end of that year he left and in the fall enrolled in, I think, The McCallie School, in

Tennessee, a school with a reputation for a good religious education. I next heard of Pat when he was in Washington and Lee University in Lexington, where he made a real contribution to the term, "a fraternity boy"! Again, as far as I can recall hearing, he didn't make many waves, he was the fraternity brother of my friend Charlie McDowell, Charlie later went on to become a member of "Meet the Press" and a columnist for the Richmond Times-Dispatch.

I recall hearing that Pat had gone into the evangelistic ministry, and I remember thinking, "that's a good job for Old Pat'! The rest is history.

In the 1990's, when Pat makes his first attempt to be the Republican nominee for President, we were invited to attend what was called, "the First Post War Reunion of the Classes of 1945-1949". We went, having attended the Alderson High School Reunions, had spoiled us.

It was good to see some of the kids I hadn't seen for many years and noting the ones with less hair and larger waistline than my own. It soon became obvious that what we were attending was a cleverly constructed device to get former Lexingtonians reacquainted with Pat, hopefully to return from whence they had came, there to form some sort of 'a grass roots movement' that would enhance his presidential hopes. It was from the outset a "religious right" evening. My wife and I left with the feeling we had been had.

I next saw Pat when he again was seeking the nomination; now just what in Pat's background would have prepared him for the Presidency is totally beyond me, but there he was, on the campaign trail. He was to speak at a breakfast in Lewisburg, the bank had been seduced into buying a block of twelve tickets and were having a heck of a time finding twelve Republicans in Alderson! Finally, they managed to fill their table by threatening to foreclose or something like that, and off we went.

Pat was working the room, I'll have to admit he is a smooth talker, when he came up to me and introduced himself, I said. "Yes, Pat, I know you; we went to Lexington High together". I then made the mistake of telling him my name, when he got up to speak, he was so lavish with happiness and joy about again being in my company I wanted to slide under the table, when he started on my football career at Lexington, (which, believe me, was not all that great), the real friends I had surrounding me, began to look at me with a quizzical expression. I maintained a very low profile in Alderson for a few weeks afterwards, I especially did not go into the bank, I did my business at the drive-in window.

Pat was, as I had remembered him, just a smoother article, and a politician much like his father but without the actual political acumen of A. Willis Robertson: Junior Senator of the United States from Virginia.

Lieutenant. Montgomery's Car

John McCurdy, '06.

In the years from 1951 to 1954 I was working at the Radford Arsenal in Radford Virginia while attending college in a nearby town. In my early twenties, newly married and a new father my desires and wants were many and the means to afford them non-existent. One of my many interests and desires was automobiles, especially sports cars since they had only recently made an appearance in this country. Little M.G.'s and Jaguar's, and indeed, any other high-performance automobile would bring goose-bumps to my skin. The great classic automobiles of the 1930's like Packard, Cord & Cadillac, of this country and the Rolls and the Mercedes of Europe were of just as great interest.

Alas, I was forced to be content with a 1940 V-8 Ford Deluxe Convertible, with brown Leather seats and a Maroon body, (a car I would today give a lot of money for). I could generally find enough money in our budget to buy the monthly Hot Rod, Motor Trend and such magazines, but there was no hope of a Jaguar in the foreseeable future. I had to be content with yearning for those possessed by more affluent acquaintances. Paul Oakey from Blacksburg, the son of the areas best known funeral director had a 1953 MG-TD, that he spent hours polishing, even taking the wire wheels into the house to lovingly wash each spoke by hand in the family bathtub.... Crazy Bob Tasch had a Jaguar XK-120 and then bought another, this one a 1952 Or 1953 Jaguar XK-150C. He would drive the road to the Arsenal through Prices Fork with the top down. Winter and summer, the top was down, he would often arrive at work wearing what appeared to be all the cloths that he possessed. I wanted to be able to be one of them!

The local Ford Dealer in Radford had, at the time, sitting on his lot, a 1936 Cord Front-Drive Roadster, the price was an astronomical $1200.00, (they now sell for over $100,000.00), I drove it, I went there and sat in it, I lusted for it! I would likely have traded my first-born for that car if that chance had been there.

I ate and I drank and I dreamed of cars and I'm sure I drove others, especially my long-suffering wife, nuts with my incessant discussion of and my passion for automobiles.

Everyone who I worked with was familiar with my love of unusual and old cars and would, when they heard of a special old vehicle hiding in a barn or as in the case of "Texie" Guyans Packard Roadster, sitting in a backyard and being used for a chicken Coop, tell me of them, I made notes and went to look for them. I guess against the day when I thought I would have the money to indulge my passion.

Sam Simmerman, a colleague in the Technical Department, informed me that a Lt. John F. Montgomery of the U.S. Army, and who was from the Pulaski area was unloading an antique car he had purchased in Europe and had shipped home. It had arrived by rail car that week and Lt. Montgomery was going to get it off of the train car and onto a truck for the trip to his home. That Saturday morning at 9:00 AM, Sam and I were at the Rail Station in Pulaski awaiting the event. The automobile was under wraps on a flatcar and was going to be rolled from the car onto the platform and then onto the truck. When the vehicle was at last safely on the firm earth, the young man proceeded to unwrap his prize and allow the throng to get a look at last.

It seemed when he pulled the cloth from the hood that the engine cowl must have been 8-10 feet long, then the windshield appeared, no top yet, hen another windshield and behind that a small cabin with only room for two. It was not clean, there was a fair amount of surface rust and a dent or two, but it was a HUGE automobile and it spoke volumes of the riches it would have taken to have purchased it when it was new.

Young Montgomery told us he had bought the car in France, that he had paid $5000.00 for the car, and a another thousand or so to get it to America, that it had once been owned by King Carol of Rumania, and that it was one of only seven ever built. It was, he said, "a Bugatti Royale" a Type 41.

It was, at last, loaded onto a truck and Lt. Montgomery drove away. The first and the only time I ever saw him or the Bugatti. I did, however, not forget the automobile and as time went by I learned more and more about the remarkable Ettore Bugatti and his marvelous creations, of which the "Royale" was merely the most costly and complex.

Ettore Bugatti was a Frenchman who went to Italy to build his automobile in the decades of the 20's and 30's. He was the Enzo

Ferrari of his day. He built huge cars like the 'Royale" and tiny cars to hold only a very small driver, but all that he built would go like "the hammers of hell" and stick to the narrow Alpine road of Italy and France like glue. His cars won every prestigious road race in Europe, he was a autocrat who cared little for money, just as long as he had all he needed, he refused to cater to his customers comfort, he refused to worry about real braking power in his automobile saying, to one prospective buyer, "monsieur, I make my cars to go fast not to stop"!. Some of his cars were so cranky that they demanded that the oil used in the engine be heated and then poured into the crankcase before the car would run. He was able to sell every car he produced; they were simply the best in the World at what they did. And what they did was get one from point A to point B faster than any other automobile ever produced.

When a very wealthy prospective buyer told him, "M'siur Bugatti, everyone knows your cars are fast but for luxury one really must buy a Rolls-Royce"! Bugatti threw him out and began planning the "Royale"!

It had a wheelbase of 14 feet, from the radiator cap to the windscreen it was 7 feet! It had a straight 8 cylinder engine of 12,760 ccs, about the size of three Cadillac engines of today! The crankshaft weighed more than 220 pounds and ran in nine individually water-cooled bearings. It would run in high gear from 3 miles per hour to over a rock-steady 125.

It sold, the chassis only, mind you; for 30,000.00 dollars in 1928! The customer then had to shell out another 20,000 to 35,000 for a custom-built body! In exchange for his money the customer got free service and overhaul for life and for a radiator ornament, a white elephant!

I don't know where the car I saw is now, however a Bugatti "Royale" holds the record for the most money ever paid for an automobile. Several years ago the last "Royale" that has been sold, brought more than the sum of $7,000,000.00 at auction in the United States at I believe, "the Nethercutt Auction" several years ago!

Nitroglycerine

John McCurdy '05

In 1953 I was a technician for Hercules Powder Company at the Radford Arsenal in Virginia. I had been in the Acid Lab for a year and then was transferred to the Quality Control department as an Inspector.   A grand promotion to $1.75 an hour!

The plant had been having problems in the production of Nitroglycerine, for some unknown reason many batches that were made were just barely within specification. Hercules was producing single and double-based powders and other product for the U.S, Government of course, and Hercules specification were always more stringent than were the Government specifications, in that way if a problem was in the process of occurring we at Hercules would be first aware of it and could start trying to determine where the problem lay.

Nitroglycerine is made by glycerin being treated with a mixture of Sulphuric and Nitric Acid in a process called Nitration, a simple explanation of a slightly more difficult chemical procedure.

We produced the Nitric Acid by a process of passing Anhydrous Ammonia

Through a Platinum Gauze in the presence of heat, afterward the weak nitric acid was concentrated and made ready for use. The Sulphuric Acid was produced in house from a very concentrated form of Sulphuric Acid called Oleum. The two were then mixed in about a 75/25 mixture, Nitric Acid being the lesser.

The Glycerine was purchased mostly from Palmolive-Peet and the Colgate Companies and arrived in at Radford in 55 Gallon steel drums. A single batch of nitroglycerine called for about 2000 pounds of Glycerine and 7000 pound of the Nitrating Acid, the nitrating tank having a capacity of about 10,000 pounds.

The Glycerine was combined in a heated tank by dumping the 55 gallon barrels, (the Glycerine had to be heated because of its viscous nature). It would then be introduced to the acid mixture in very small quantities with special attention being paid to the attendant temperature rise in the Nitrating Tank, (the tank was cooled by a brine and ammonia mixture circulating through the walls of the tank. After the entire batch of Glycerine was used and it had been washed and de-acidified several times it as ready to use. It was now Nitroglycerine.

Samples were taken in rubber bottles about 6 by 1 inch, about like the delivery hose on gasoline pumps, plugged with a rubber stopper and placed, in a small wooden carrier outside the immediate area where they would be picked up. The individual picking them up would be on foot and would then carry them to the Nitroglycerine Lab, a building separated by considerable distance from other buildings for rather obvious reasons.

When the problems with the product became evident, additional samples were taken, but the reasons remained a mystery.

Senior Technician Kelly Webb from the Powder Laboratory and I were asked to accept a special task to trying to get the root of the problem. We were promoted to a new position at the hourly rate of $2.00 per hour!

A Spent Acid Tank about equidistant from the Nitroglycerine Area and the Powder Lab was chosen and on top of it, about four stories up, our new laboratory was built. A wooden frame-work was erected around the top, a wooden floor put in and numerous windows of Plexiglas placed in the walls. Electricity was run up the side and a few bare light bulbs provide our new home with night-time illumination. An anemic electric heater attempted, with little success, to keep the place warm. An open outside stairway with a 2X4 railing led from the ground to our workplace. When the cold wind blew off New River we knew it!

At the beginning of each shift, we would have to carry a supply of ice up the stairs for use in the testing procedure. A large flat area that was actually the top of the tank was our laboratory workbench, no toilet, only cold water, a very Spartan workplace. We had a supply of large beakers to hold the ice for the tests, a bunch of 250ml. Erlenmeyer Flasks, pipettes and burettes and thermometers and rubber sample bottles and an Analytical Balance to weigh the samples and ingredients. $150.00 would have bought it all but the Balance! We were not a first class operation, In fact, we were cheap!

Over the next few months we sampled everything imaginable used in the production of Nitroglycerine, we would use the acid mixtures and samples from each individual barrel of Glycerine, the acid in a small beaker in a large beaker of ice, the Glycerine in a burette slowly dripping into the acid while we stirred with a thermometer to make certain the temperature didn't go critical. Then we would send the sample we made to the Lab and wait.

We sampled weak acids, concentrated acids, every thing but fingernail clippings, at the end we had not found any single reason for the problems, but almost, as if by magic, everything fell into place, the nitroglycerine was within specs again and the problem disappeared and they allowed Kelly and I to descend from our perch and join again our friends on the ground!

It was the consensus of the mighty that it was inattention to detail that had been the cause of the problems and when it became known that we were checking everybody and everything; people started tightening up on the procedures.

Kelly and I were both promoted as a result of our work, (or ordeal), in the next year I went into the Federal Prison Service. It looked at the time like a safer way to make a living!

My Ancestors played with Guns

John C. McCurdy

I know there has been much discussion about whether or not little girls like dolls and such things and whether boys like to get muddy and play with stuff like trucks and toy guns as a result of something in their very nature or if it comes about as a result of expectations of them.

I really don't know and if you want to know the truth; I don't care! In my opinion the way it is, is fine.

I can remember that as a kid, the nice soft dirt under the back porch or the sticky wet clay of a creek bank was my idea of a perfect play area. The roadways and tunnels my pals and I made were much more real than any parent-supervised activity of today. Matter of fact, the last thing we kids wanted, was grown-ups around, grown-ups only hindered a fellow.

You think about it, about your own childhood days; adults were in truth, a nuisance, they had this thing about dirt, and grass stains and cockle burrs and beggars-lice, about fighting and throwing rocks and clods, about B-B guns and gravel shooters, and cussing!. If adults had their way we would have learned about the difference in the sexes from an adult, instead of in the barn from cousins and kids down the street!

Our parents seemed to be quite content for us to check in every-now and then, they knew they could expect us sometime around supper-time, lunch was whatever and where-ever we happened to be.

My Dad's family was farmers and stalwarts in the Presbyterian Church of Rockbridge Baths, Va., prosperous and well-fed; they had no particular interest in games or such distractions as fishing and hunting. The idea of shooting a rifle or a hand-gun just for the sheer pleasure of doing so. My guess is there was not a hell of a lot of fun in them, they not only professed their religion, but they lived it as they thought meant for them to do; working, saving, churching for the Glory of God!

My mother's ancestors, the Coffey's and the Fitzgeralds and the McCormack's were another story all together. They were mountain folk, happy to be left alone on the crest of the Blue Ridge just to the East of Lexington's gentility. They also were farmers but their land was less productive than that in the rolling farmland of the Shenandoah Valley below. They timbered and trapped and hunted and fished and some of them made moonshine, they were Baptist, Methodists, Presbyterian and when they veered from "The Way", they fretted about doing so, they did not necessarily do any thing about it, but they fretted about it!

They took their lumber and agricultural products and the furs they had trapped to the James River and to the B&O Railroad to go to the city that might as well be on the other side of the world, to Lynchburg and Richmond! They hunted to provide variety in the meats and to supplement the almost steady diet of fat back- and other parts of the hog. Venison, squirrel, game bird and rabbits were a welcome change. Is there anything better than Squirrel Gravy and Biscuits?

Shooting matches, in which one would see who could put his bullet nearest the "X" made by a sharp knife on a slab of wood, with money or merchandise prizes for the best Marksman, serves to encourage one to do a little practicing in the back yard.

In a closet under the stairs in my Granny Fitz's house in Alderson there were always rifles and shotguns. They were just part of a well-equipped household. A single -barreled 12 gauge shotgun and a well-used rolling-block Remington .22 caliber rifle. There was another .22, a Remington slide-action repeater, broken and beyond the capabilities of the local Gunsmith to repair.

The back side porch of the house overlooked a valley of vacant land and my uncles would stand on the porch and shoot at targets, generally tin-cans, in the yard below. I recall one instance when they made a bet, (I think it was for a million dollars), as to who could hit a marble, on a slice of moldy bread, that they had sat on the post of my Gran's clothesline. To everyone's surprise the first shot hit the marble and blew it to smithereens, the second Uncle said he wasn't going to pay up!

I would be allowed, under close supervision, to shoot occasionally, and on every opportunity would go to the closet and look at the magic guns just waiting for me to be old enough to use them.

There were never any guns in my own house until my Mom, one special Christmas, gave my Dad a Remington .22 caliber bolt-action repeater, with peep-sights and a 6-7 shot clip. It was beautiful. I was ten years old. Dad was a very good shot, I don't remember that he ever hunted; he did love to shoot at cans and bottles in the nearby trash-dump. I remember he used it each fall to shoot the hogs we raised for food; they would always drop without a peep, or rather a squeal. I was allowed to do the shooting one fall, with terrible results, the poor pig ran squealing around the hog-lot and one of the men assisting with the butchering had to finally throw himself on the poor pig while another man cut the throat of the pitiful animal. I learned a lesson of life on that autumn day.

That Christmas I received a boy's greatest compliment, my own rifle, it told me that my parents felt I had the maturity to use and own a device with tragic potential; I was in Heaven that Christmas morning. A little Montgomery-Ward Western Field single-shot .22 made by Mossberg.

It would have been even more wonderful if I had received cartridges, and understanding parents had tucked two boxes of .22 shorts in my Xmas Stocking!

I still have the rifle, or rather I know where it is safe, I cut the stock and barrel to fit my oldest son, he used it and in turn my grand-son and perhaps even my great grandson. I am sure it will be well taken care of.

I have owned many very expensive and very accurate rifles and pistols since then, but none comes close to taking the place in my heart of my Dad's bolt-action Remington or my precious Montgomery Ward/Mossberg .22 caliber rifle.

The Coal-mining Years

John McCurdy 05

In 1939 or there about my family moved to a small settlement near Point Pleasant. Five or six miles further up the Ohio River and into the hills of Mason County several miles to a wide place in the road called Kaylong. My younger brother and I attended a one room school known as Locust Grove, 30 or so students made up the   8 grades that were combined in the single room.

My Uncle Ed Fitzgerald, my granddad Adolphus and my father were in the business of coal mining! It is my memory that Uncle Ed owned the farm on which the coal was located and that my Granddad and Father were the owners of the mine, paying Uncle Ed a royalty on the coal that was removed.

My family and Granddad lived on opposite sides of the mine. Granddad in a two story house with a drive in garage-basement. We lived in a smaller house beside a little brook on the opposite side of the mine works.

Across the narrow, dusty dirt road ran in front of our houses was an old abandoned mine open to animal and small children alike. Fascinating and frightfully dangerous! Nearby on the same side of the road were several houses even smaller than ours. The men of the families living in them were all workers in the mine.

Carl Bryant was one of those men. A short, ruggedly handsome man about 40 years old he and his wife and son lived nearest to us. There was a much smaller house/shanty behind the Bryant house, another employee of the mine, a bachelor named Sam, about 60; lived there and took his meals with the Bryant family.

Carl Bryant had been a club boxer when younger and I was fascinated with him, he unfortunately had a habit of going on a drunken binge periodically. On these binges he would invariably get into a brawl and be put into jail in one of the surrounding towns. My Dad or Granddad would have to go pay his fine and get him out of jail in time to work on Monday morning; his fine would then be deducted from his next paycheck.

He came home from one of his outings, quite drunk and quite belligerent. Poor old Sam was sitting in the kitchen of Carl's house eating his supper as he did every night. Carl accused Sam of making advances to his wife! Sam's denials were of no avail! Carl threw Sam from his house and began to beat him terribly. He would knock him down and when Sam tried to get away crawling, Carl would stand him up so he could hit him several more times before he fell again.

My mother heard the commotion and screamed for my Dad to "make him stop', "DO SOMETHING MAC" she urged!

A length of two by four about 4 feet long lay beside the fence, Dad put it over his shoulder and marched over and across the road to rescue Sam. My Mom was now yelling, "Mac, don't go over there, don't go over there"! However my father walked into the Bryant yard and told Carl if he did not calm down he would surely bust his head. I think Carl knew my father well enough to realize he meant what he said. He was reduced to bluster and threats but took no more violent action.

Dad took Sam over to the bath-house of the mine and in the nearby blacksmith shop water-bath cleaned and patched Sam up, and put him to bed in the mule barn on a pile of hay.

He went back to the Bryant house and told the still-raving Carl to come with him. He then took Carl over to the mine and locked him in the building next to the Mule Barn, telling Carl to calm down and go to sleep or else. I don't think either of them were sure what the "or else" was to be.

Both Carl and Sam were incapacitated until late Sunday night; both were at work Monday and acted as if nothing had happened. Dad never answered my questions as to what he would have done if the threat of the 2 by 4 had failed. However I was convinced he would have done just what he said he would.

A Day in the Life of a Kid

John McCurdy 2005

Charlie and I had started about 8 o'clock that morning, on my almost new bike I had zoomed down from my granny's house on Kieffers Hill and into his yard just in time to catch him coming out of his back door wiping the sleep from his eyes while his mom was yelling at him to come back in and eat his breakfast. We went back into the house and had a bowl of cornflakes with a banana and milk.

We then made our rounds of the Post Office lobby and the phone booth on Main Street where we once found a dime in the return slot. Talked to Dave Coleman on the Post Office loading dock about the boat he was going to make for us when we had saved enough money. Dave was the kindly freckle-faced colored man, (yesterday's description), who was the janitor at the Post Office. We went into Peg or Pecks Grocery and checked to see it they were hiring and they weren't and then next door to his Dad's furniture store. We helped cut a piece of linoleum from one of the large rolls and helped Willie Fawcett, load it into the customer's truck. We left before anyone wanted us to sweep up and strolled down to the Alpine and reviewed the posters of upcoming attractions at the movies.

It was the July of 1942, I was 12 and Charlie was 11 years old! The War was 6 months old and we were getting licked by the

Japs in the Pacific! Saturdays at the movies we saw the news reels of the battles that had take place weeks before, even the newspapers lagged behind the actual events a week or more. We loved to see the path of the tracers arching out into the Pacific Sky! Little did it matter; we knew only what we could comprehend. We were not really affected.

We went to the depot, Mr. Dameron was kind to kids, and we bought a gum-ball from his machine and then walked the tracks back up to the bridge and hung over the parapets looking for fish in the river below. A visit and a walk around the Funeral Home, with a long, serious discussion of the things that went on behind the shaded and draped windows until such talk gave us goose-bumps. We ate our lunch at the insistence of Mrs. Nelson and Aunt Stella at their kitchen table and as soon as we could head to Elinor's house.

Elinor was my sweetie, kinda! Seeing as how I had given her a genuine imitation diamond just a week or so before. It had been in the top drawer of the buffet in my Grandmothers dining room, a leftover from some ones past. Elinor was a year older than me and light years older in many ways, as girls generally are. We immediately got as far away from the grownups as we could, we went to the wash-house and got our swim suits, making a big production of trying to be modest, but making sure that we all got good looks at the other twos naked bodies . We had dammed the little creek flowing from Dark Hollow and made a private swimming hole. Charlie and I got into a fight as we did at least once every day and Elinor got mad and went to the house and Charlie and I cursed each other and threw clods and went our separate ways.

In a few hours he showed up at my house and we had a bowl of brown beans and home-made bread and butter to sustain us until supper. We adjourned to the clubroom, (our basement) and read old magazines for an hour or so. For some reason we decided to go to his house, probably because no one was there at that time of day. His dad was at the Post Office working and his mom was at the Store and the colored lady Ossie, who worked for them, would have gone home for the day. Charlie had to take a crap and so I sat one side of the tub and helped him and then we went to the basement. We smoked some rabbit tobacco rolled in newspaper and then Elinor showed up.

We tried to get Elinor to take of her clothes but she shyly refused , I don't know why since normally it she did not view it as a problem, as I recall Charlie offered to give her up to a dollar. Where he was going to get the dollar was any ones guess! Since Elinor did not want to fool around we went upstairs and into the yard in time for an interrogation by Junior Lobban and Bruiser Foster. When Junior and Bruiser were unable to get Charlie and I to fight, they decided we needed to know how to play football with the emphasis on tackling .One of us would run around the house and the other one was supposed to tackle him as he rounded the corner. I'll admit Charlie was better at it than I, I wanted to evade the opponent, A trait that made me a fairly decent running back in High school but a poor fellow to have on the defense.

Junior and Suicide got tired of us quickly and told us to hit the road. We drug a stick on the picket fence of the house next to Aunt Stella Nelson and journeyed over to Bill Clifford's house, Bill was not home, probably a good thing because we generally got beaten up when we hung around with Clifford. We got the seine that always hung on the side of his barn and waded the creek looking for hellgrammites to sell to Minor Bare, having no luck there we decided to try our luck with Elinor again with the same results as before. When we went to Copeland's Garage and asked Bub Bare if they had any old ball bearing we found the welcome mat had been rolled up for the day, they guys were washing up and getting ready to go home, so we decided that's what we would do, we had had a pretty hard day.

John McCurdy 04

In the early days of the Federal Reformatory for Women at Alderson and indeed up until the late 40's or early 50's the female Correctional Officers assigned to the residence cottages worked rather odd shifts. The Cottages all, at one time, had kitchens and dining rooms and the inmates assigned to that cottage ate their meals in what was considered their home.

The officers would come on duty at 2:00PM and supervise the cottage, including the preparation and serving of meals, after cottage cleanup and the evening leisure hours of the inmates she would, after they were safely locked in their rooms for the night, do a safety and security check of the cottage interior and only then could she go to the Offices Bedroom and bath.. There to retire for, hopefully, a uninterrupted nights rest, however if problems arose in the cottage she had to take action. In the morning she would awaken before the inmates and start them in the day's activities , generally making the first pot of coffee and then awakening the kitchen help. After the breakfast was over and she had gotten the women out for their work assignments she would supervise the Cottage maintenance women in cleaning and polishing until she was relieved at 2:00PM..

In the late 40's, an officer (a Ms. Farley) was fired and she decided, after consulting with an Attorney, that the Correctional Officers were being short-changed in the hours they were paid for. That since they were required to remain in the cottage for 16 hours they should be paid for 16 hours!

The now former employee engaged Peter J. Beter, an attorney from Charleston, West Virginia ; to represent her! Lawyer Beter recognizing that there would be many other officers who were in the same situation , took the case for a contingency fee of 33 ½ %!

Beter began, with the aid of at least one or more employees, to solicit other officers to engage his firm to represent them in an attempt to receive renumeration for the hours they had been required to be in the cottage, even if they were sleeping or at least in the officers room.

The case was heard in the Sixth District Federal Court, and the court did find that the employees were entitled to back pay for the hours between 10PM and 6AM when they were required to be in the cottage.

The Business office had a monumental task going through old, dusty, pay records and time sheets and determining the amounts owed to the employees both current and long-gone! The Staff was divided, the individuals who had joined in the suit had their renumeration reduced by the Attorneys fee and the other staff members also got back pay but since they had not sued had no obligation to Mr. Beter. Some resentment has lingered for years. The total sum of the "BACK PAY" was approximately $6,000,000.

The American Federation of Government Employees was the fledgling

Union representing the employees. It was essentially toothless, but several of the union officers actively solicited other individual to join in the suit and as a result their careers were damaged, some quite severely.

Frost-bitten fingers and near drowning in the frigid waters of the creeks around Mill Point if they had only made a few more dollars they would have almost broke even!

I fished and I hunted with Bob Craft, we biked into the Cranberry wilderness and we camped, and ate half-cooked bacon and blackened eggs in the rain. and once or so we shared the cup. I think we respected and enjoyed one another's company.

Bob sometimes had a head that could be as hard as a rock, and at times he could be a cantankerous cuss, but all men can, as you ladies can attest. Once we were young and going to live forever, it doesn't seem to work that way and so once again I say goodbye to a friend.

Bob Craft was a decent, honorable, good man, full of life and a lover of life. A good husband and father, a lover of the outdoors, of the smell of newly sawn wood, and of burning leaves and banjo music. A shy and humble man. He was most

of all a Gentleman and a Gentle Man.   We should all do as well
with our lives!

Have You Ever Really Been Frightened ?

John McCurdy '04

The frenzied barking of the dogs of the neighborhood awakened me, they were normally well-behaved dogs not bothering anyone and certainly not disturbing their sleep. There was a snow on the ground and a moon that kept peeking from behind the dark clouds that were racing across the sky. At the dogs insistent barking I got up and went into the bathroom, the night-light on the clock showed 4:PM. I did not turn a light on as I went to the kitchen where I could see nothing that looked out of place in the back yard but when I looked out the kitchen door I saw that 50-60 feet up from our gate a car was parked.

I assumed it was lovers who had taken advantage of our dead end lane as often had happened in the past. I had at one time several years before stepped onto the porch with my 1911 .45 and emptied a clip of eight into the flower bed. The "thunk" of hears hitting the car ceiling was a joyful one to me. I was tired of having to pick up the signs of their visit and as I had several times in the past, I decided to take action. I got my flashlight and slipped out the door. The neighborhood dogs were barking more wildly than ever as I walked up to the car from the yard side of the fence. I shone my light into the interior expecting to see a surprised and likely very embarrassed couple. I was surprised to find the car was empty. I turned and began to walk back to the house, when suddenly to my surprise, the lights came on, the engine roared and the car shot by me with the wheels spinning and scattering gravel behind. I shone my light into the car and snarling at me from the window were two ferocious mastiffs with bared teeth and hatred in their red eyes. I couldn't figure how someone with such beasts could have gotten into the car so fast, I didn't get a clear look at the driver just an impression of a person dressed on dark colors. When the car passed I was too stunned and surprised to get a good look at the license plate. The only numbers I think I saw were EVIL---666!

I wondered why the cars exhaust smelled so much like sulphur. I entered the house. I closed and locked the doors and then I sat in the living room and waited for daylight.

Family Traditions - Lost Treasures

Copyright 2011

Carter Taylor Seaton

I'm ambivalent about automatic dishwashers. It's not that I don't appreciate their value to today's busy households; it's just that I've long wondered if we've lost more than we've gained by their introduction to our kitchens. Indeed, one of my fondest memories revolves around the days before dishwashers.

While washing dishes was a task I grew up trying to avoid at home, I longed to engage in the camaraderie that surrounded it at my grandmother's house. Being fairly well off, she had a maid who normally cooked and washed the dishes, but after special family gatherings, my grandmother often did them. She had a huge country kitchen with a brick patterned linoleum floor that even I knew, at six, was fake. A double sink directly under the kitchen window split the only countertop in half and held a toaster on the right and a dish rack on the left. This long, uncluttered expanse of Formica allowed plenty of room for stacking clean dishes, once they'd drained briefly. The large wooden table that dominated the center of the room served as the resting place for the dirty dishes.

Sunday dinner was over. My grandmother had cleared away the heavy damask cloth and matching napkins and repositioned the silver candelabra with its graceful curling arms in the center of the heavy oval table. All was in order in the dining room, but the mess now covered the kitchen table and the task of restoring order had begun.

Her maid, Lucy, scraped the plates of their vestiges of mashed potatoes swimming in gravy, bones of fried chicken picked clean and the stray pea or two left by a child who hated them. One plate had an entire serving of peas artfully tucked under the napkin; as if its owner hoped this hiding place would escape his mother's notice. Lucy had a rhythm all her own; with one foot she'd step on the pedal of the trash can. The metal top would pop up, she'd slide in the remains, move her foot to get the next plate, and the top would clang shut. She repeated the ritual until she worked her way through the huge stack. She salvaged any leftovers in the bone china serving dishes for tomorrow's lunch or tucked them away to take home that night. The actual dishwashing fell to Mother and my aunts, Elinore, Nancy, and this Sunday, Margery who was home for a long visit.

Dressed in their nearly matching Sunday-go-to-meetin' dresses, Margery, Nancy and Mother looked like an arbor of cabbage roses. Elinore disdained such a frivolous frock and instead wore a straight linen skirt and short-sleeved sweater. My task was to help by drying the silver, although if it had been to scrub the garbage pail, I'd have done so, just to be with them. Standing on a step stool so I could reach the counter, I felt part of the sisterhood. As the precariously tall pile of dirty dishes shrank, the steam from the sink fogged up the kitchen windows. While Nancy washed and Elinore rinsed, Margery, and Mother dried the glasses and the dishes, and I tackled the silverware. Linen tea towels, too soggy to be effective, hung limply on the backs of chairs as new ones appeared from the seemingly endless supply in the drawer to the left of the sink.

The singing seemed to begin with Lucy who hummed when she wasn't talking. When the monotony of the task and the joy of ending the day's chores loosened the old black lady's tongue, she began to sing an old gospel song. Her rendition of "The Old Rugged Cross" was enthusiastic but off- key, for she couldn't carry a tune in a bucket. Of course, I didn't know that, so I just chimed in and matched her note for note. So did my aunts, whose own pitch was less than perfect.

Once Lucy had finished her chores, my grandmother let her go home early, it being Sunday, and we finished the dishwashing. At Lucy's departure, the musical repertoire took on a decidedly secular slant as first one, and then another sister took up a song. Elinore led off with a fraternity drinking song from Duke whose entire stanzas (the butchered version of an old Irish ballad) didn't make it back from North Carolina, like –

'Oh, the night that Paddy Murphy died,

I never shall forget.

We all got stinkin' drunk that night

And some ain't sober yet.

The only thing we did that night

To fill our hearts with cheer,

Was take the ice from off the corpse

And put it in our beer!

Nancy, in full voice switched to the chorus of,

"Don't go in the lion's cage tonight, darling mother

For the lions are ferocious and they bite,"

She could never recall the verses, so she would switch to:

"Have you seen my blue eyed Sally?

172

She lives down on Shinbone Alley.

Number on the house; number on the door;

Next one over is a grocery store.

Stay all night; stay a little longer.

Take off your clothes and throw 'em in the corner.

Don't see why you don't stay a little longer."

And Margery offered,

"'Twas a cold winter's evening, the guests were all leaving

O'Leary was closing the bar.

When he turned and he said to the lady in red,

'Get out, you can't stay where you are.'

Oh, she wept a sad tear in her bucket of beer,

As she thought of the cold night ahead.

Then a gentleman handsome, peered over the transom

And these are the words that he said.

'Her mother never told her,

The things a young girl should know.

About the ways of college men,

And how they come and go, mostly go.

She's lost her youth and beauty,

And sin has left its sad scar.

So remember your sisters and mothers, boys and

Don't let her sleep under the bar.

That old brass rail.'

As we got to the last refrain, we'd belt it out with off-key gusto.

Dishes washed, dried, and put away, I'd reluctantly leave the quartet, who would soon follow. As the door swung open into the dining room, the spell was broken and I was a six-year old kid again, no longer part of that intimate gathering. Knowing, however, that we'd be back another Sunday, I'd skip happily to the cozy living room to sit with the others.

Therefore, it's no surprise that my delight in discovering a Kenmore dishwasher in our newly purchased home in 1961 was tinged with sadness, as it dawned on me that my infant daughter might never share my experience. In fact, she might not even learn how to wash dishes. As I rocked her in our dark living room in the middle of the night, I imagined that from now on, all homes would probably have dishwashers. People would never experience the camaraderie of sharing song, intimate conversation, or gossip as they washed their family's dishes. They'd simply stuff them in the giant mouth of the metal marvel and flip a switch. I agonized over this as she grew, although as a busy mother with four children, I was not inclined to take the extra time to show her the finer points of dishwashing, or singing.

I need not have worried. Dishwashing seems to be a skill we learn, even if by osmosis. When she was a young mother with two small children, I often saw her wash her share of pots and pans, even if her dishwasher did swallow most of the dishes. Moreover, when I walked into my daughter's home recently as she was showing her three-year-old grandson how to rinse the dishes before putting them in her dishwasher, I thought, "now all she needs to do is teach him to sing."

The Lost Literature

Serena Quillen 2017

It had been five months since Aunt Emma died. My cousin, Shirley, had asked me to come over to Mayport and help sort out her things so they could be divided between us cousins.

It was a hot July day when we went. After a short visit, she and I agreed that we would split duties and we drew cards from an old deck on the side table in the parlor, as Aunt Emma called it, to see who would go up to the attic. I drew a five and Shirley drew a nine, so I got the attic. She tackled Aunt Emma's bedroom, while I took the stairs to the upper landing where the attic access ladder was.

Mayport, like all of its surroundings, is hot in July. The attic was not well ventilated and it was stifling up there. I promised myself when I got up there to only spend about ten minutes before going back down. I found an old trunk that was full of stuff and I got Shirley to help me lug it back down the ladder. I tied a rope around the handle on one end and held onto that to lower it while Shirley supported it from below. Together we still only had a tenuous grip on the thing, but we got it back down to the second story landing. The rest of the stuff in the attic was mostly junk: an old broken floor lamp and a winter coat that had been well worn.

I was soaking wet and sweltering by then, so I took off my blouse and slacks and sat in my underwear on the bed and opened the trunk. From the dust in the attic, it appeared that the trunk had not been moved or opened in quite a while. I let the remaining dust fall from the trunk lid to the bedroom floor, where it could be easily vacuumed up. The trunk had several garments in it, night gowns and underwear, mostly. In a neat stack in the corner, were about twenty paper backs. I got them out in groups of four and five and spread them out on the bed. They all appeared to be romance novels and I did not think anything peculiar about them. In the bottom of the trunk was an old cigar box, wrapped with a strong red rubber band. I picked it up and tried to roll the rubber band off, but it broke as I began. There were three stacks of letters, each held together by yet another red rubber band. One stack in business envelops was addressed to aunt Emma, as second stack in smaller envelopes was also addressed to Emma and the other to a Wade Simpkins, with a Post Office box address here in Mayport. I wondered why she would have and keep a stack of letters addressed to someone else, and I noticed that they all had been mailed and delivered and opened. I pulled the contents from the envelop on the top of the stack. In it were a letter from Emma to Wade, which I put aside, and a note from Wade to Emma.

"Dear Emma,

For security reasons, I am sending you all the letters you sent me over the years. I have kept them hidden in a secure place and no one has seen them but me. We are leaving tomorrow for Duke Hospital and my surgery is scheduled for next Thursday. There will be a lot of testing beforehand and I expect to be in the hospital for a while after the surgery. In case I don't get to come back, I wanted you to have these letters. I know you will know what to do with them.

Thank you for all the tenderness you have shown me over these last few years. If I do not come back, you can rest assured that my last thoughts were of you.

Wade."

The date on the post mark was three years ago.

Emma had been a widow for fifteen years. Her husband, Lewis, had been killed in a slate fall in the Dobson number eleven mine, along with eight others. All of us cousins remember going to his funeral. We were from nine, or so, to seventeen years old then. Now the seven cousins would split Aunt Emma's estate. There could not be much to it, though. A two story frame house on a quiet street in Mayport, a nine year old Ford, some furniture, a small checking account and a savings account and an insurance policy with a face amount of five thousand dollars.

By now, I was curious, so I picked up the other stack of letters and took them over near the window. Once I determined that the tree outside gave me the privacy I wanted, I opened the window and sat on the other side of the bed to read the other stack of letters. These letters were addressed to Emma with no return address, but the postmarks were all Mayport.

Rainbow Dreams

The waif-like young woman crouched beside the railroad tracks on the outskirts of a small West Virginia town was barely visible in the pre-dawn fog that shrouded the entire valley. She stared into the mist expectantly, as if awaiting a lover's arrival. Her dog stood and began to whine as he felt, rather than saw, the train glide to a stop near the water tower. The girl shifted the heavy backpack to get under it more squarely and then began to move purposefully toward the train. As the husky matched the girl's quickening pace, his red neckerchief flashed. At the end of the coupled cars sat the back engine, which she knew from experience most likely would be empty. She grabbed the railing of the steps, pulled onto the platform, took two steps upward, and watched anxiously as the agile dog sailed like an acrobat to the lowest step. Reaching down, she gave his head a quick pat. The train had barely hesitated before it began to lumber down the tracks and into the deepening fog with two new passengers in its cold, empty cab.

As she slung the backpack to the floor with a quick shrug of her shoulders, the dog followed her every move, checking to be sure they were settling in before he sat beside it. Under a buckskin vest, she wore a flannel shirt and beneath the matching buckskin skirt, thick woolen leggings. Although spring was coming, even the morning air was still cold enough to frost her toes. The red bandana tied around her head didn't exactly match the one around her dog's neck, but it was close. Her soft leather boots looked like Robin Hood's and the knife handle protruding from the right one implied a formidable blade below. First, she removed the tarp, then a tattered Army surplus blanket from around the backpack, and spread them in sandwich-like layers on the cold metal floor. A second smaller blanket she rolled into a pillow and after eating the piece of jerky she'd pulled from her shirt pocket, she crawled between the layers. The dog moved closer and sat sentinel-style at her side.

As the train slipped rhythmically through the morning, she felt her mother's arms around her, warm and comforting. "We'll be there, by and by, sweet-pea. We'll be there by and by," she sang, rocking the thin three year-old. She could hear her saying, "Read the sign, sweet-pea. S-T-A-T-I-O-N. Station. That's where the train stops, but we're staying right here. Just a few more stops, then we'll be in Louisville." As her mother's voice faded, a deep growling one took its place and a frown clouded the girl's face. "Get in the cellar, you little bitch. When I tell you to do sumthin, you do it! I'm yer pa now. So, stop yer sniveling. If you run again, I'm gittin the switch." His voice suddenly softened and his hands were on her. "Now, ain't that better? I jest want to kiss you, pat you, love on you a little." She jerked upright, a look of panic on her face, and stared through the dusty half-light as if the voice might take shape and find her again. Immediately, the dog stood, barking sharply. "It's okay, Trash. I just had a bad dream." She lay back on the makeshift pillow, but sleep wouldn't return; the image of the man and the musty, dark cellar were still too vivid.

She rose, squatted beside the backpack, and withdrew a dog-eared, cardboard-bound composition book, and a stubby pencil. On a clean page she began, "Dear Virgil, It's early morning and I'm headed to Louisville, then on out west. I want to stop to see Mom's grave before I leave the east. I know she ain't there, but it makes me feel better to talk to her. Last night I met some musicians who talked me into singing one of my songs at a concert they was giving. 'Course I cleaned it up a bit. I was embarrassed and happy at the same time. I never done that before, but you'd have been real proud because the audience applauded a lot. I sang one I'd written a couple of weeks ago but haven't sent you, so I'm gonna put it down here.

"Well, hey there railroad copper, I see you in your truck.

You don't want me on your freight train, well, but I don't give a fuck.

You don't want me in your boxcar. You don't want me in your yard,

Or lying by the railroad tracks smoking my cigar.

You don't want me in your coal bucket or in your forty-eight.

You woke me in that gondola and said get off my freight.

Well, hey there railroad copper, I see you in your truck.

You don't want me on your freight train, well, but I don't give a fuck.

You don't want me riding power, cranking up the heat

Or lying 'neath the brakeman's seat kickin' up my feet.

Don't want me on your pig train, blowing in the breeze.

Arrested me for trespassing on railroad property.

Well, hey there railroad copper, I see you in your truck.

You don't know I'm on this hopper car and I don't give a fuck.

When I wrote it, I'd just outrun the railroad bulls in Clifton Forge. I know if they catch me now, I'll be in real trouble because they've got my picture. But don't worry; I ain't going back there.

Virgil, I can't wait till you get out. We'll go set up in the woods like we've planned since we was kids. I'll get off the rails, we'll get some land, and you'll never get locked up again. When you can't sleep at night, think about what I think about when it happens to me. I remember going to sleep with the stars bright above and waking in the morning dew to find deer all curled up in the grass across the clearing. It don't get better than that, does it? Well, I'll close now and write again after Louisville. Love, Sister"

The Norfolk and Southern crept into New Orleans as if it were hauling elephants on its gondolas, yet only the thin girl and her dog disembarked a few blocks shy of the station. The train soon went on its way and the pair headed purposefully toward town. Later that night, as Pizza Hut was closing, they waited patiently in the alley. Soon a pimply-faced boy wearing a Saints' ball cap and a tomato smeared apron tossed several boxes in the alley dumpster. As he disappeared, the girl scrambled up its side and retrieved two of the boxes. They smelled of pepperoni and oregano. She stuffed them into the backpack and motioned for the dog. Several blocks away on a park bench, she ate the still warm meal. As she gave a piece to the dog, a shy looking black girl, older perhaps, but not by much, approached, staring with unconcealed envy at the seated girl. "You hungry," the diner called out. "I've got extra." The black girl reversed her direction and dropped eagerly on the bench. "I didn't eat today, so I thanks you," she said. They talked a little as they ate, then the black girl rose, said thank you again, and left the park.

The next day, after asking for directions from several folks who seemed eager to get away from her, she walked to the Ninth Ward to see for herself the devastation of Hurricane Katrina. Although several years had passed, she was not surprised to see houses still boarded up with big red Xs spray painted across the front. Her disdain of government had prepared her. Later, near the French Quarter, a panhandler caught her eye, and the hair on the back of her neck prickled. Although she hadn't seen him since, she was sure it was the man from whom she'd barely escaped with her life. The abuser who had dragged her across the country for four years, and who mercilessly raped and beat her each time she tried to escape. The man whose van she finally jumped out of on I-56 when she realized he was going to kill her and dump her in Maurepas Swamp. It wasn't the same dog he'd had back then, but the hunch of his shoulders, the shoulder length greasy hair, and the way he sidled up to his marks, were the same. "Holy shit," she thought, walking quickly in the direction opposite the one she'd originally intended. "I thought he was back east." Careful not to attract his attention, she didn't run until she was several blocks away, then she and the dog gathered speed, jogging as fast as the heavy burden on her back would allow. She would have hitched a ride, but that was almost as scary. Too often men wanted "payment" for a ride and she wasn't about to give them what they wanted. She had stopped taking that chance long ago. They were both out of breath when they reached the tracks outside of town.

The westbound was waiting, silent and still in the gathering dusk, it was shorter than the train on which they had arrived. Quietly, she hoisted the dog into an open boxcar near the rear, and then climbed in behind him. Exhausted, she lay down to wait for the train to leave. "What the fuck do you think you are doing?" The railroad cop was on her before she awoke. He grabbed her by the arm to pull her to a standing position. She resisted, curling into a ball that she hoped gave her body more weight; but he kicked at her shins, striking her hands, and her legs. Trash began to growl and lunge at the man, who was tough, wiry, and mean looking under his billed cap. He turned, without releasing the girl, and kicked the dog in the ribs with his steel-toed boot, sending him yelping and flying across the boxcar. Then he kicked the girl again, grabbed her arm, and twisted it behind her, pulling her upright. As she fought to get loose, he punched her in the temple and her nose began to bleed. The dog tried another attack, and the man pulled a pistol. "Don't," the girl yelled. "I'll come with you." He put away the pistol, and slapped her again, as he muttered, "That's more like it."

The next day, after using all the money she'd saved from shoveling snow last winter to bond herself out of jail and Trash out of the pound, they trudged away from town stone broke. "Well, Trash, strike New Orleans off our list. We won't be coming back here again." Suddenly, she stopped, reached down, and scratched the dog behind the ears. "Poor Trash, I'm sorry he hurt you." The girl turned her face to the clear sky for a long moment, then lowered it and said, "Just wait, one of these days, we'll have our place in the woods. Just you, me, and Virg."

In early spring, when life began to reappear in the scrub sand around Texas, the cactus once again looked fat and succulent, their blossoms beginning to show yellow, pink, or red. Even the giant saguaros bloomed, their flowers dwarfed by the arms that hosted them. They would fade in the hot summer, but for now, they were beautiful. Prairie dogs and armadillos sunned themselves on flat rocks and the border patrols, also warmed by the sun began to search more diligently for illegals.

When Sergeant Ray Williams, opened the door to the second engine of the parked Burlington Northern freight near El Paso, Trash began to bark. The girl, sitting under the brakeman's chair, tried to jump past him, but he grabbed her. A look of shock crossed the Sergeant's face. "Dammit, didn't I tell you last year

184

to keep your butt off this train? I knew I shouldn't have let you go with a warning. This time, you're going to jail." She stammered, "Come on, Sergeant. If you let me go, I really, really promise not to come back. I wouldn't have done it this time, but I've been sick and couldn't work enough to earn the fare." "Bullshit," he thundered. "You've never paid a fare in your life. How many warrants do you suppose there are for you? Enough to keep you locked up for a long, long time, little girl."

He jerked her arms behind her and locked on the cuffs, pinching her skin in the motion. She yelled, "I can't go to jail; I can't stand being locked up. What about my dog?" "Fuck your dog," he said. The Sergeant grabbed the girl's pack, and as he did, the composition book slid to the ground. He walked roughshod over it as he manhandled her toward his pick-up. Trash followed his mistress, growling and trying to nip at the man as they moved. Shoving the girl into the pick-up first, he slammed the door and got in on the drivers side, leaving Trash behind. "I want my dog," the girl screamed. "Don't leave him. He's all I've got." The cop started the truck and drove away without a word. Twisted in her seat, the girl watched Trash running after the truck until he was lost in the distance. After the Sergeant looked up her record – finding a plethora of un-served arrest warrants – she was booked and put in a cell at the county jail.

She sat on her bed bunched into a ball, her head on her knees, her eyes swollen and red. The smell of all the cell's former occupants assaulted her nose – sweat, urine, and tobacco – and reminded her of another crowded jail in a midwestern town whose name she didn't remember now. What she remembered vividly, however, was how desperate she was to get out; how she'd have done anything to be back under the open sky; how the claustrophobic cell reminded her of that cellar in her past, especially in the darkness; how she'd found the white powder in a hole behind the toilet; how she'd thought it was a bag of drugs left behind by some other jailed soul; how she'd eaten it and nearly gagged from the bitter taste, but didn't care, wanting to forget where she was; and how she'd awakened in the clean, white hospital after they'd flushed the rat poison from her system.

Cold sweat dampened her bandana and she began to pace. Twenty steps across and twenty back. She counted them over and over. She pressed her whole body against the barred door and breathed deeply, hoping for fresh air, but none came – only the acrid scent of cigarettes burning in the distance.

She yelled at guards she couldn't see but knew were there, "Where's my dog? Why did he leave him behind? That cop had no right. Please go find my dog." From down the corridor came a guttural voice. "Shut up in there." Returning to the bed, she curled up again and rocked.

Late in the evening, she asked for some paper and a pen, which they brought her. "Dear Virgil, I'm on my way west and just wanted to say hey. It's warm and things are beginning to bloom. As we rode into town, it was raining lightly and I saw a double rainbow. I made a wish on it – that you and I would soon be together in the woods. I don't know if rainbow wishes work, but I thought it was worth a try. I probably won't stay long because it will get too hot, but when I come up the coast, I'll come see you, then head north again for the summer. Take care of yourself, and I'll see you soon. Love, Sister."

She lay down, staring out the tiny mesh covered window. A full moon was showing in the center, as if it were shining for her only. Forgive me for the little white lies, Virgil, but I don't figure it would help to tell you I'm in jail too. A television flickered silently on the shelf above her head. She turned to the wall and slept. Five deer – a doe and her fawns – walked in a circle, mashing down the grass until they had it soft and spongy, then they knelt and slept. In the tree, an owl hooted softly. Stars dotted the sky like diamonds tossed from a croupier's cup. She

186

saw Virgil and Trash emerge from the tent to look at the moon, and she rose to greet them.

"Good God, we got us a hanged girl," one of the guards yelled. "Come help me get her down." The television screen was black, but the moon illuminated the cell like a Klieg light. She swung slowly from a beam, a faint smile on her lips, the red bandana askew on her head.

The Why Bookshop

Michael Connick

I unlocked the front door of the bookshop and flipped on the lights. I inhaled its unique odor with notes of coffee, chocolate, and even a hint of vanilla in the air. I had come to love the distinct smell of my shop. It was the first anniversary of my ownership and I recalled that old quote, "If you want to make God laugh, tell him your plans." How apropos for where I now found myself.

Two years ago I was a police officer in Los Angeles. I loved my job. I got to drive fast, carry a gun, and put bad guys in jail. I planned on serving a full thirty years on the job. Then the accident had taken all that away.

I had been in pursuit of a teenage car thief when a truck with an inattentive driver slammed into my patrol car. The firefighters needed to use the jaws of life to cut me out of my cruiser. I spent two weeks in intensive care, followed by three operations to repair the damage to my lower back and pelvis. These weren't enough to fully restore my mobility so I had been granted a medical retirement from the LAPD.

The next months were hell. I'd been a cop all my life. It's all I had ever wanted to do. At 6' 4" and 200 lbs, I had always been an imposing physical figure and stayed in great shape. My mere appearance could take the fight out of most of the people I needed to arrest. Now at the age of thirty-five I was a pitiful cripple in constant pains who needed a cane to walk.

So, I just stayed at home, watching TV and playing video games. I drove my girlfriend away when I couldn't take her pity anymore.

I took too many pain pills and supplemented them with too much alcohol. Late at night I sometimes broke down and cried, and then drank enough to pass out.

I was at that terrible point where I thought I would soon eat my gun when the certified letter arrived. It was from a lawyer in West Virginia. I was born in Charleston, WV, but my family moved to Southern California when I was three. I hadn't been back to that state for almost twenty years. What the hell did a lawyer from there want from me?

The letter informed me that my fraternal grandmother, Alisha Casto, had died and left me a house and a bookshop. They were free and clear of all debt and were mine to do with as I pleased. The only problem was that they were located in the little village of Why, population 2800, in the southern part of West Virginia.

I had to look up Why on the internet to find where it was and how it had gotten its odd name. Turned out it was called that name because of a trick of geography. It was located at the junction of two streams which came together to form a small river. On the map that junction of waters formed a perfect letter "Y", and so the village that grew up there took on the name "Why". It was in the poorest part of the state, an area of played out coal mines.

What the hell was I going to do with these white elephants? I decided to go to Why and check them out firsthand. I might be able to find some local who had just enough money to take them off my hands. I would be happy to sell them cheaply.

My grandmother had been a nurse for most of her life in Charleston, WV. For some incomprehensible reason she had retired to the remote village of Why. There she bought and renovated a beautiful old Victorian home, complete with two-story turret and widows walk on the roof. She also had a new building erected to house a bookshop. Grandma had poured her entire life savings into these projects.

The bookshop seemed to be the focus and real love of her life. She spent virtually every waking hour there. At its center was a roomy open area containing couches and comfortable chairs. Any resident of the area was welcome to stop by and sit a spell, trading local gossip and enjoying free coffee from the pot that Grandma kept brewing all day long. Actual book sales were pitiful, barely covering operating expenses, but the Why Bookshop was the heart of this tiny community. It was the closest thing the village had to a community center.

I felt trapped. It would be heartless to close the bookshop, it seemed so important to the little town that was enduring decline and severe economic hardships. It was also a living monument to Grandma's work in bringing hope and enjoyment to this depressed community.

No one in the area seemed willing or capable of taking over the bookshop. My monthly pension from the LAPD was a kingly sum compared to the typical income of the town's residents. It really wouldn't cost me anything - moving to Why would actually save me money. I would no longer have to pay rent and the cost of living there was a tiny fraction of LA's. So I ended up moving into Grandma's house and becoming the not so proud owner of the Why Bookshop.

My first duty on opening the bookstore that morning was to get the coffee pot going in order to continue Grandma's tradition. I thought about getting a cake later to help celebrate my first year at the bookshop. Jake walked through the front door just as the coffee finished brewing.

Along with the bookshop and house, I seemed to have inherited Jake Masters. He was not very intelligent, but he was a hard worker and a gentle, kind soul. He had dropped out of high school at sixteen after spending most of his life in Special Education classes. That was right at the moment when Grandma had become old enough and frail enough to need some help around the shop and her house, so she hired him. He had worked faithfully for her for the last five years of her life.

Jake had keys to both places and continued to maintain the properties after Grandma died. He knew more about the business than I did at first. Since I also needed help with the physical aspects of working the bookshop and maintaining the house I just kept him on. He was serving me just as faithfully as he had Grandma.

He cheerily greeted me as he walked into the bookshop. "Good morning, Mr. Casto." I had long ago given up trying to get Jake to call me Jeff. He had called Grandma "Miss Casto" and I would forever be "Mr. Casto" to him.

"Morning, Jake. I came in yesterday so there's some trash to take out of the office. Could you take care of it?" The bookshop was open from Tuesday to Saturday, but I often came in on Mondays to do paperwork and pay bills.

Jake hustled off into the office and then out the backdoor carrying a trash bag. A large dumpster sat in the alley behind the shop.

I slowly limped back to my office, carefully adjusted my chair for minimal discomfort to my lower back, and started up the store's computer. I had just started going through email when I heard the backdoor open again and Jake softly say, "Mr. Casto, please Mr. Casto, he's hurt bad.".

I got up and walked out of the office to a sight that caused me to gasp. There stood Jake with a large bloody knife in his right hand.

A young man lay dead in the alley, covered in blood. I took the knife from Jake and dropped it into a large Ziploc bag from our small kitchen, taking care not to get my own fingerprints on it or disturb any that might be there. I led Jake into my office and told him to wait there until the police arrived to interview him.

I called 911 and the Why Police Department quickly dispatched a car to the scene. I had met most of our local officers and had not been impressed by the tiny eight-man police department.

Sergeant Glenn McCrum was the responding officer. I knew him slightly. He had visited the bookshop on particularly cold days while on patrol and taken advantage of our free hot coffee. He seemed a decent enough guy.

He took a quick look into the alley and then called for one of the Sheriff Department's detectives. Forty-five minutes later, Detective Ralph Gandee arrived. He was a large heavyset man who wore a brown cowboy hat, a shabby gray suit, a gray shirt that must have once been white, and a stained black narrow tie. He smelled strongly of aftershave.

Gandee quickly surveyed the scene and came into the shop. I brought him to the office to speak with Jake. He took out his notebook and said, "So, Jake, what happened here? You know the victim?"

Jake swallowed hard. "Yes, sir, that's Tod Oldaker. I was in school with him."

Gandee licked the point of his pencil and wrote something in his notebook. "Why did you stab him?"

192

Jake turned to face me and shook his head. "What does he mean? I didn't stab him. I tried to help him. I saw he was hurt bad, and I saw the knife sittin' on the ground next to him. I talked to him but he didn't answer. I asked him if he was OK but he didn't say nothin back. I picked up the knife to show it to you. I figured you'd know what to do with it."

He then turned and looked at Gandee. "Why you think I stabbed him? I ain't seen him since we was in high school together. I got no reason to hurt him."

Gandee asked a few more irrelevant questions and then left to go back into the alley. He had told Jake to stay right where he was.

A Sheriff's forensics team arrived later in the morning and took Jake's clothing and the knife into evidence. They left Jake wearing a white Tyvek suit and still sitting in my office. They also carefully searched and photographed the entire scene. Finally, Sheriff Martin Queen arrived on the scene in full uniform. He was taller than me and extremely thin, looking positively cadaverous. I wondered how he had managed to get elected as our county's Sheriff considering how unattractively malnourished he looked. He immediately ordered Jake arrested for murder.

I protested vehemently and he turned towards me and snarled, "Look, Mr. Casto, you may have been a big shot in LA, but here you're just a bookshop owner. You keep your nose in your own business and we'll just get along fine. Otherwise, I see big trouble for you coming down the pike."

Jake looked like a whipped puppy as they took him away in handcuffs and he stared at me with pleading eyes. "Help me, Mr. Casto, I didn't do nothin."

What the hell was I going to do now? I couldn't believe Jake had killed the man. Where could he have he gotten that huge knife? It was a chef's knife at least ten inches long. He hadn't been carrying it when he went out the backdoor of the shop. All of this made no sense.

He would not do well in jail. He was not crafty enough and far too gentle. I also had very selfish reasons for helping Jake. I needed him. My injuries prevented me from doing the physical work of shelving books and moving boxes around the shop. Jake was my strong back and legs. He also mowed my lawn and tended my yard. I was helpless without him. I had to get him released as soon as possible. Otherwise, he'd spend months in jail awaiting trial.

The fastest way to get Jake out of jail was to find the real killer of Tod Oldaker and deliver him on a platter to Sheriff Queen. So, that's what I was going to do.

The next morning I saw Sergeant McCrum slowly driving his cruiser down the street in front of the bookstore and I flagged him down. "Glenn, can I talk with you for a minute?"

"Sure, Jeff, hop in."

I shook my head. "Sitting kills my back. I spend all my day at the office using various cushions and pads on my chair trying to get comfortable. Even standing still hurts a little. I'm most comfortable when walking, even if I do have to use a cane to steady myself. How about you get out and go for a brief walk with me? You can walk a beat for a few minutes, can't you?"

Glenn laughed and got out of his cruiser. We started walking down the street. I noticed that Glenn kept his head on a swivel, constantly looking at everything going on around him. He was a better cop than I had given him credit for.

"Glenn, Jake didn't do it. Can you help me prove that?"

"Look Jeff, I like Jake, but it's out of my hands. The Sheriff investigates murders in this county. I don't even know what kind of evidence they're putting together against Jake."

"OK, fair enough, how about telling me all you know about Tod Oldaker. You've lived here all you life, haven't you."

"Yeah, I sure have. Well, Tod was a real piece of work. In school he was a notorious bully. In fact, I've heard it said that Jake quit high school primarily because he had been so badly bullied by Tod. That's not going to help Jake's case."

I sighed. "What else do you know about Tod? What's he been into recently."

Glenn took a moment to check the lock on the door of an abandoned business we were walking past before replying. "Nothing we can prove, but I think Tod was dealing drugs. The town has been awash in meth lately and rumor has it that Tod was the main source. He may have had a lab somewhere back in the woods outside of town."

Meth? That's a mean drug and meth heads are notorious for violence. Had one of them killed Tod? That seemed far more likely than Jake doing it. I needed to look into this. "So, tell me how I can find out more about Tod Oldaker and especially about his drug dealing."

"Now Jeff, you don't want to be interfering with the Sheriff's investigation. You're going to get yourself into a whole pile of trouble. Sheriff Queen is not a man to screw around with."

"Yeah, I'm sure he isn't. So, tell me where Tod Oldaker lived."

Tod Oldaker lived in a double-wide trailer about fifteen miles outside of town. I decided to close the shop for the rest of the day. Why could get along without their community coffee pot for a few hours.

In spite of how uncomfortable it was for me to ride in an automobile, I did own one. It was a huge black Chevrolet Suburban with a diesel engine and four-wheel drive. I had bought it strictly based on how the driver's seat felt to me. It was the least uncomfortable one I had been able to find. I had also added some additional lumbar support to the seat so that driving this giant vehicle wasn't too painful for me.

I limped back to Grandma's home. In the garage sat my Suburban, which I had named The Beast. It was a boat to drive and swallowed diesel fuel at a prodigious rate, but it did come in handy when hauling books. It could carry a seemingly endless number of boxes of books effortlessly when pressed into such service.

I pulled myself up into the driver's seat, set my cane on the passenger seat, and fired up the diesel. The always reliable engine started immediately and I headed out toward Tod Oldaker's trailer.

Upon arriving there I encountered "crime scene tape" across the driveway, but no law enforcement vehicles were on scene. It looked deserted.

I pulled The Beast right up to the crime scene tape and parked. I'd get out and walk around the property and then check out the trailer and see if I could get inside it. The walk would help my back. Even with the special seating arrangements I'd made in The Beast, driving any distance in it always gave me a little discomfort in my tailbone and stiffness in my lower back. A short walk would help relieve them both.

The property was a mess of weeds and overgrown vines. The trailer was rusty and one of its windows was covered over with a plywood sheet. Tod Oldaker was not living the life of luxury you would expect from someone manufacturing illegal drugs. I wondered where all his money was going, certainly not into this dump.

I walked around the back of the trailer when I spotted a four-wheeled ATV. It looked new and well kept. Maybe it was the one piece of property that Oldacker was proud of. Its engine suddenly made a ticking sound, like it was just cooling off. I walked over to it, and sure enough it was warm. Someone had ridden it here. I was not alone, after all.

I felt immediate regret. I had no handgun on me. As a retired police officer, Federal law gave me the right to carry a concealed handgun almost anywhere. I had my duty Glock and a compact FN pistol locked away at the house. Why was such a quiet little village I'd gotten out of the habit of carrying a pistol. Even the compact pistol was pretty heavy to carry and put a strain on my back.

Just as I turned to walk back to The Beast the back door of the trailer opened and a man stepped out. He was wearing jeans, a denim jacket, a flannel shirt, and motorcycle boots. He had long stringy black hair and red blotches all over his face. He smiled and I saw a mouth full of rotten teeth. He was definitely a meth addict.

He put his hands on his hips. "Well, well, well, what do we have here, a gimp? What you doin here, gimp? You looking for the money? Terry's going to be very, very pissed off if you're trying to steal it from him. Or do you already have it? Give it to me and I'll tell Terry what a good boy you've been."

He stepped towards me with his hand out to grab my arm. I didn't have a gun, but I did have my cane. At the hospital, I had been given a cheap aluminum cane. My good friend Greg was an instructor with the LAPD and he had told me to throw it away. He gave me a new one. It was a self-defense cane.

It looked like a regular wooden cane and even had the rubber tip on its end. However, it was made of extremely hard wood and had small grooves cut all along the shaft. These permitted me to get a slip-free grip anywhere on it. Greg then taught me two cane fighting techniques. He assured me I'd only ever need these two to successfully fight off any attacker. They were the Thrust and the Two-Handed Swing.

As the guy got within five feet of me I whipped the cane up with my right hand, put my left on top midway down the shaft and thrust the end of the cane hard into the man's solar plexus. He made a "whoosing" sound as his breath was driven out of him. He stopped, bent slightly forward, and grabbed his stomach with both hands.

I then moved my left hand down to my right wrist and swung the cane back. I whipped it forward as hard as I could with both hands and hit the side of his left leg just above his knee. The blow caused a "crack" as loud as a gunshot. I thought I had broken the cane, but what was broken was his leg. He cried out and fell to the ground.

My back was screaming in pain from the effort I had put into hitting him, but otherwise I was OK. I looked down at the guy and said, "OK, what money are you talking about, and who is Terry?"

He screamed, "Screw you."

My back really hurt now, so I was in a very bad mood. I poked my cane onto his broken leg. He screamed even louder and I yelled, "If you don't answer me right now, I'm going to break your other leg and then start on your arms."

He just moaned in response, so I started to raise the cane back over his right leg. He shouted, "No, no, I'll tell you whatever you want. The money's fifty grand that the scumbag who lived here stole from Terry, Terry Valentine, for some meth. Except he never delivered the meth and Terry is very, very pissed. He killed the weasel, but he still wants his money back. He sent me here to look for it, but I tore the place apart and can't find it anyway. Look, if you know where it is, Terry may give you a finder's fee."

He started sobbing and tears poured from his eyes. I actually felt sorry for this wretch of a man. "One more question: where is this Terry Valentine right now?"

He stopped crying and looking scared instead. I raised my cane again. "No, no, don't hit me again. He's at the shithole motel in Why. Room 24. He'll kill me if he knows I told you. Please, don't tell him."

I shook my head. "No, I won't tell him. I am going to have a little talk with him, though. He's gotten a friend of mine into a whole lot of trouble and now he's going to get him out of it. You just stay still and I'll call an ambulance for you. You move that leg around anymore and you may never walk on it again. When it comes to broken bones I know what I'm talking about."

I headed back to The Beast. When I got inside I called 911 as promised, and then headed back towards Why. I was going to need to have a heart to heart talk with Terry Valentine, but I needed a plan. I couldn't just go into his room and bash him with my cane until he promised to confess. Something more subtle would be needed. Plus, I desperately needed to go home and take an 800mg Ibuprofin. The pain in my back was becoming unbearable..

Early that evening I knocked on the door of room 24 in the Why Motel. A large muscular man with shaved head, huge silver chain around his neck, and wearing jeans, a Taylor Swift T-shirt, and a leather vest answered the door.

"Mr. Valentine?"

He turned his head and said, "Boss, visitor."

Terry Valentine was a refreshing change to the low-end fashion scene I'd been experiencing all day. He was a short man, probably not more than five and half feet tall, but impeccably dressed in an expensive looking white shirt, a Christian Lacroix tie, and what looked to be custom tailored slacks. His hair was jet black and worn in a pompadour. Here was a man who believed in doing whatever it took to look well-groomed and well-dressed. He stood in stark contrast to the Taylor Swift fan he shared his room with.

Valentine stared at me intently and then said, "Come in please, what can I do for you?"

"Let me cut right to the chase, Mr. Valentine. I'm Tod Oldaker's very, very silent partner and I want to thank you for dealing so effectively with that little shit. I also want to repair the damage Tod did to our business relationship."

Terry Valentine was sitting on one of the two double beds in the room. He showed no expression on his face in response to Tod Oldaker's name. He said, "Jason, please check out our new friend for weapons and, most importantly, a wire."

Jason roughly grabbed my arms and Valentine spoke harshly to him. "Gently Jason, you don't want to hurt him, at least not yet."

Jason then continued his search of my person in a more gentle manner. It was extremely thorough and turned up nothing.

Valentine reached for a glass and took a sip of what looked like Scotch. "So, if you are Mr. Oldacker's partner, then you owe me $50,000. I want my money and I want it now."

Suddenly his face was reddening and he opened the drawer next to the bed and pulled out a twin to the chef's knife that had killed Tod Oldaker. He seemed to be losing control of himself. I had to speak quickly and calm him down before he stuck that knife into me. Jason was now close behind me and put his meaty hands firmly on my arms, pinning them against my sides.

Valentine now spoke in a low growl. "You think I'm some kind of pussy? I want my money or your guts in my hands right now."

He stood and advanced towards me. I had to think fast about how to defuse this situation. It was quickly spinning out of control. "You can have your money tonight, or perhaps something even better. What did Tod promise you? It must have been a very sweet deal for you to pay in advance of receiving the product. I can offer you just as sweet a deal and this time deliver it. What I want is to repair the damage Tod has done to both of us. Let's both get rich. What do you say?"

Valentine now held the point of the huge knife right under my chin. I felt it prick my skin. I was a dead man. I closed my eyes and prepared to die.

Then Valentine pulled the knife away and laughed. "You must think I'm a complete moron. You want to tell me another pack of lies. I'll tell you what I want from you. I want my $50,000 or five pounds of Ice and I want them right here in this room tonight."

Five pounds of crystal meth for $50,000? That was quite a deal in rural West Virginia, more than enough to convince someone risk some upfront money on the chance of getting so much product at so little cost. Of course, Valentine was probably lying, jacking up the amount Tod had promised him for his money. It really didn't matter at this point.

"If you'll get this goon off me I can get you your five pounds tonight. I want you to have the product. You did me a huge favor by killing Tod. He was getting out of control and sampling the product himself. Then he tried to ruin our business by ripping you off. You deserve the five pounds just for solving that problem for me."

Valentine looked me intently in the eye for a moment and then said, "Jason, let our new business partner go. So, Mr. Silent Partner, what's your name? Or do you prefer to continue to be silent?" Valentine laughed at his own joke.

"My name is Jeffrey Casto, Mr. Valentine."

"Now when do I get my product?"

"I can go get it right now. Jason can come with me if you'd like. One thing before I go though. Tell me, did you make Tod suffer when you killed him? Did you make him squeal?"

Valentine gave a hearty laugh. "He squealed alright when I shoved the knife into his gut. He squealed like a little girl."

I smiled and said loudly, "OK Glenn, it's showtime."

The connecting door to the next room came crashing off its hinges and Sergeant Glenn McCrum, carrying a 12-gauge pump shotgun, lunged into the room yelling, "Everybody freeze. You get down on your knees, You too, Taylor Swift. Get down on your knees and keep your hands up where I can see them."

The Why Police Department didn't own any sophisticated recording equipment, so Sergeant McCrum had just duct taped a microphone connected to a laptop he borrowed from his son to his side of the thin motel wall. This crude rig successfully captured our conversation and because of this evidence Jake would be released from the Southwestern Regional Jail the next day. Turns out the Sergeant is actually a great cop.

I drove The Beast up to Holden to pick up Jake, accompanied by his widowed mother. I'd never met her before, but Sergeant McCrum assured me that I'd enjoy the drive to Holden in her company. Looking into her deep blue eyes and hearing her lilting voice, I had to agree with Glenn. I was definitely enjoying her company and was already thinking about how I might be able to enjoy it again in the near future. It looked like I might be inheriting two members of the Masters family, and I didn't mind that at all.

www.ingramcontent.com/pod-product-compliance
Lightning Source LLC
Chambersburg PA
CBHW030323180626
46810CB00003B/1214